SHARPSHOOTER'S AMBUSH!

The noonday sun was tipping onto his left shoulder when Adin Webb saw dust boiling to the east and realized it wasn't a dust devil but Old Anse Pickard bouncing around on the high front seat of the approaching stagecoach. Unhurriedly, Webb tamped the large leaden slug into the long barrel of the Ballard & Lacy and sat down on the hunting seat behind his rock cairn.

"Easy," he murmured, squinting into the scope, "let them come a little closer."

Clear as if they were close enough to shake hands he could make out Old Anse, the sunburnt texture of the skin in the seamed face wreathed by a watchful grin. Webb made the decision to place his scope's reticle on Pickard's right breast, since it was his considered opinion the wind would carry the round to the right six to eight inches.

"Another couple of seconds," he murmured again, "and that's all she rides."

MONTANA RIMFIRE

ROBERT KAMMEN

ZEBRA BOOKS
KENSINGTON PUBLISHING CORP.

ZEBRA BOOKS

are published by

Kensington Publishing Corp.
475 Park Avenue South
New York, NY 10016

First printing: January, 1991

Printed in the United States of America

Chapter One

The man clad in homespun butternut could feel the menacing presence of a Union patrol fading away into the foggy patches of thick woods. Still he waited, keeping a short grip on the reins, his ears keened to the dying thud of shod hoofs.

It was early May, by the reckonings of Adin Webb, the fourth day of this warm spring month. And just after sunrise, but still with a few eerie shadows lurking under the thick and seemingly endless trees comprising the northern edges of the Wilderness. Here the mist lay thick and dewy on thickets and trees budding into life. He welcomed its embracing cover, knew that he would have to move out before long and take that gambling ride across higher and open ground spilling up to a rocky hill. Most likely, he mused, that cavalry patrol would be equipped with one or two field glasses. Though Adin Webb figured it was highly unlikely anyone would think to look back. For they were looking for bigger game than a lonely Reb sharpshooter.

They were looking for the leading remnants of Lee and the Army of Northern Virginia. Other patrols were out, as he'd managed to avoid them in his ride up through this vast hunk of stunted trees and impenetrable underbrush. His orders were plain, daring: lay his gunsights upon General U.S. Grant. He knew the Army of the Potomac was camped not far from the old battlefields of Fredericksburg and Chancellorsville. Now under him the chestnut, a horse he'd conscripted from a farmstead just this side of the Virginia line, switched its tail and farted, which caused him to mutter, "What I think of them damned bluebellies."

The sharpshooter hailed from Taney County in southern Missouri, a place of bald knobs shelving down to the White River. Webb had been eeking out a living as a small sharecropper, as his father had done before him, when war erupted to divide the country. Soon afterward Union troops moved into the region, and like most, Adin Webb simply gathered up a few provisions and his rifle and hunted out a place to join the Confederate army. He fought at such places as Chickamauga, Bull Run, and Shiloh, and then to be picked as a sharpshooter and sent out to kill and forage behind enemy lines.

The man from Taney County did not have that lean and hungry look as others of his deadly craft, being somewhat hefty through the middle, with folds of loose skin under his dreamy blue eyes, the round face thatched at the moment with a two days' growth of black stubble. He more resembled a quartermaster clerk or cook. But as it turned out Adin Webb seemed born to this lonely trade of killing men from afar. By his estimate, twenty-three bluebellies had run afoul of his sharpshooter's rifle. Further, Adin Webb had the singular ability to forget the eyes of the men he'd sighted in on through the telescope attached to his killing weapon, to brush aside any stirrings of remorse. To him it was a matter of pride when a single bullet took out a Union soldier, and at distances up to a half mile or more. Most often there was this brief look of surprise, for the unlucky bluebelly never heard the report of the rifle that had killed him.

Webb spoke to the chestnut. "Let's quit this lallygagging . . . and make for that knoll." Gently a booted heel brought the horse out from under the brooding trees.

His unexpected appearance brought a few birds fluttering out of oak trees and shrubbery clutching at his legs. But he kept heading across the clearing and to where it swept upward. Here there were scattered trees and mossy rocks larger than both horse and rider, the chestnut laboring up with a slow, choppy rhythm. He found the top of the rocky hill to be fairly level, while it gave him a clear sweep of the land to the north, with Adin Webb seeing for the first time, the army commanded by General Grant spread out to overflow a valley. He hadn't realized he was this close, and with this sudden knowledge came a slight tremor of fear.

"Can't be more'n a mile," came his wondering murmur as Adin Webb gazed at orderly rows of tents and soldiers and caissons, while here and there were flags and guidons marking the different Union Corps. He realized there would be more enemy units farther to the north and maybe spread out to the east. By rights what he should do was come about and bring the exact location of the Army of the Potomac back to General Lee. No, that was the task of Jeb Stuart's light cavalry, and other scouts sent forward to seek out what the bluebellies were up to.

He got down heavily, a tired man in his early thirties, to bring the chestnut back around a boulder and tie the reins to a low tree limb. Untying his canteen from the saddle, he pulled out the cork while taking in the mellowy blue sky filled with patches of cloud. How serene it looked, maybe with a few angels keeping watch over both armies soon to converge in battle. Though he had no misgivings about carrying out his duties as a sharpshooter, Adin Webb knew that Gettysburg had marked the turning point of the war. The Cause, as all Reb officers liked to call it, was doomed by the northern armies with their unlimited supply of arms and men. He felt that the war would soon be over, and he had no intention of surrendering or living in a defeated South. By rights he should have headed west through Tennessee instead of coming here, perhaps to suffer an inglorious death. He did not fear the thought of dying, as this was part and parcel of his bloody business. The dread in Adin Webb was that with the cessation of hostilities his killing services would no longer be needed. There came a certain inward release when his bullet found human flesh, a deep joy filling his heart, a truly pleasurable moment that not even whiskey or a willing woman could give him. Yes, came his silent admission, he truly enjoyed this killing game.

Now he drank sparingly, letting another chord of remembrance drive away the task at hand. Like all believers in the Cause, he'd been outraged when news came of Lincoln's Emancipation Proclamation. There was this newspaper editorial, in a Washington City newspaper he'd come across, stating that no longer did southern negroes have to flee to find freedom, that now it was their masters who left to escape from the "Linkum gunboats." This last statement was a refrain from a Northern song. With a derisive smile poking through the stubble, the sharpshooter from Taney County in Missouri sang gently, scornfully: "De massa run? ha, ha!

De darkey stay? ho ho!
It mus' be now de kingdom comin',
An de year ob Jubilo!"

Bitterly he recorked his canteen, felt a sliver of warm morning air brush gently against his face; an angel's touch.

"De year of Jubilo? Could be this battle will mark the end of Lee's army as a fighting force. But whatever happens, it's Jubilo time for this Missouri son once I've taken out that Yankee general."

The canteen strapped again to his saddle, a McClellan taken from the dead horse of a Union officer, he ducked under the neck of his horse and began unbuckling the leather scabbard encasing the sharpshooter's rifle. The rifle was heavier than those issued to soldiers of the line, had a longer barrel, but the sharpshooter handled it easily in his farm-worn hands. He took a clean rag out of a saddlebag and used it to wipe the film of dust away from the barrel and long stock as Adin Webb ambled past a boulder and laid his eyes upon a flat shelf of rock—that would be his firing bench. Removing the protective covers from both ends of the attached telescopic sight, he went to his knees, bellied down with the muzzle of the rifle pointing northward. He made himself comfortable by worming around so that his elbows were propped at an angle, and now he laid a caressing hand under the front stock, the other going of its own accord down to the trigger guard, and with his left eye tucking in against the back lens of the telescope.

With eye-blinking rapidity the telescope seemed to sweep the distant army encampment closer. He knew by rote the Union Corps making up the Army of the Potomac. But to sight in on an army of this size, even for a man of his calm manner, was unnerving. Directly to the north he could make out the familiar black hats of the Iron Brigade, troops belonging to John Reynold's First Corps. East of this, horses picketed behind a stone wall; could only be Buford's cavalrymen. Horses were being saddled, and Adin Webb knew that before the sun came up hot and blinding to the east, Buford's column would be moving into the Wilderness to spearhead the advance of the Union troops. He pivoted slightly to take in still more officers clustered by tents being taken down, farther to the north to a grove of elms and the hated

Yankee flag fluttering outside a stone house. It came to the sharpshooter then with a quickening of heartbeat that he was the only Reb this close to Grant's army. Grant could be in that stone house, or maybe just some other generals.

What about the lay of it opposite? Crouching backward and up from the rock, he sighted in on the southern reaches of this jumbled mass of swamp and tangled forest. It just could be he'd be caught between both armies. But it was far safer being up here than one of those slogging through hip-deep mud. He quartered the rose-tinted horizon, saw movement, grimaced at a whooping crane rising from dark stagnant water.

"No question but they'll be here. Maybe tomorrow: Lee and the whole Reb army to slug it out with the bluebellies. What had he heard just before leaving, that it was Grant's intention to march through the Wilderness in an attempt to turn Lee's right flank, and maybe force the Confederates into a decisive battle. But leave all of this to the generals.

When Adin Webb settled down on that flat rock again, the telescope revealed still more Union infantry pouring out of the bluish haze to the north, still somewhat disembodied in the uncertain light of day as if a headless snake seeking someplace to hide.

"But where in tarnation is Grant?"

That question went unanswered for Adin Webb through the endless May day. He ate sparingly of what he had, the remnants of a rabbit and what beans there were left in a can. Only as a last resort would he try gnashing his teeth around that hardtack, a piece of square food so hard soldiers had busted their sidearms in an attempt to piece it down into chunks that could be digested. Anyway, hunger was something he'd learned to control, that, and the fear of being out here alone. Toward nightfall he brought his horse off the height by a southern route. He found a stream filled with greenish water, and there was grass for the chestnut. Resisting the temptation to make his camp upon a carpet of verdant grass, since he knew to do so would mean probable discovery by a passing Union patrol, he sought that hill again.

Long before morning something told the sharpshooter the army he fought for was closing in. During the night he'd kept his telescope darting amongst the many Union campfires in an attempt to locate General Ulysses S. Grant, knew as false dawn brought a pale color to the sky that his chances were diminishing. Later, perhaps an hour, ground shadows were lifting, that now he could tell the Union army was poised to move into the Wilderness, toward him, and beyond him the Confederate army. He didn't need his telescope to make out infantry units spreading out, that before too long the order to move out would be given.

Rising, he brought his rifle to the back edge of the elevation, to suddenly discover that the army he fought for was spread out and moving northward through the Wilderness, and he muttered worriedly. "I figure they'll converge upon one another in a couple of hours or so. And here I be . . . eyewitness to it all. Angel, guard this Missouri son today. But where's that damned Grant?"

He went back and regained his shooting position on the flat rock, knowing that other sharpshooters were trying to get Grant in their gunsights, and that at this juncture in time, with both armies coming onto this killing field, any bluebelly general would do to kill. He brought an impatient eye gazing through the telescope and upon that stone house, to have his yellowed teeth click together in a pleased smile when some officers came out the back door, a major, a light colonel, then another dark blue coat adorned with two stars on both shoulder tabs. He had his general, not Grant, but one important enough to have commandeered that stone house for his headquarters. The distance he'd calculated yesterday and now this morning as being just about a mile, a hellish long shot, but there was always the element of luck. Anything could throw his aim off, heat waves, him using the wrong windage on his sights, the wind picking up to thwart his killing effort.

"But there's no wind now, bluebelly."

Through the telescope he watched the Union general unbutton his blue tunic, then remove it and hand it to the major. The general smiled as he pulled down his red suspenders and let them dangle. Then he turned to the wash basin and reached for the dark yellow bar of soap, his back to the south and the eyes of Adin Webb.

"Sight on the head . . . and if I'm right . . . should hit him where them suspenders vee on that bluebelly's lower back."

Adin Webb drew in a steadying mouthful of chilly morning air, felt his finger tightening on the trigger, eyed the crosshairs centering on the back of the general's head, and then his sharpshooter's rifle bucked. The leaden slug sped through the distance of about a mile, with the sound of the rifle a distant wail of unleashed fury, the slug punching into the general's lower back to drive him forward at the small hand mirror perched on the window sill. When the general fell heavily, Adin Webb allowed himself a pleased smile.

"No year ob Jubilo for you, bluebelly."

Quickly he went back to his tethered horse, only to discover that to either side Union infantry was inching toward the south, and that he was trapped. Farther to the south he could make out gray uniforms responding to the scattered fire of forward elements, some infantry but mostly cavalry. A glance northward showed him Union artillery beginning to pound away at the approaching Rebs. Then in the fear of what was happening his horse reared and tried to bolt away. If it did, bluebellies would be coming up here, and without hesitating he unleathered his sidearm and shot the chestnut in the head, let it drop out of sight between two boulders.

For two days the Battle of the Wilderness raged on. Troops from both armies stumbled blindly through the forest, where cavalry proved useless and artillery did little better. Underbrush caught fire, and wounded men died screaming in the flames, with both sides losing heavily, and with Adin Webb holding his lofty position until on the afternoon of the second day there were no Union soldiers blocking his westward passage.

"You have served your purpose," the man from Taney County said to his sharpshooter's rifle, and knowing that it was too heavy to carry for any length of time, that if he were spotted by the bluebellies, the rifle could sign his death warrant. So he dropped it into a thorny thicket, and armed only with his canteen, sidearm, and blanket roll, Adin Webb began the long and arduous trek that would take him to his place of Jubilo.

Chapter Two

A lot of anger rode with Charlie Siringo in that Denver & Rio Grande passenger car just passing out of Wyoming. Now he spent some of that anger crumbling up the telegram before flipping it out an open window. Here he'd spent the last four years tracking down the Wild Bunch only to be summoned back to Denver. He discounted having sent lesser members of the outlaw gang to prison, knowing that it would have been only a matter of weeks before he'd have Cassidy and that Sundance Kid behind bars.

"Wasted all that time."

"Pardon me . . ."

Charles A. Siringo, a field operative for the Pinkerton Detective Agency, shaped a cold smile for the inquisitive eyes of the man seated facing him, to have Siringo mutter, "Just unclogging my throat."

"Yes . . . it is a rather dusty day," he said uncertainly, only to have Charley Siringo gaze out an open window, and with this uncertain truce continuing until their passenger train heaved into the large railroad yard at Denver.

Gathering up his only piece of luggage, Charlie Siringo found the forward door of the car and the steps leading down to the large crowded platform. He had cold, inquisitive eyes and the leaned-out appearance of a cowhand, which he'd been in such places as Texas and Kansas. Siringo's only weapon was the silver-plated Colt .45 leathered under the knee-length brown coat. The black Justins were worn and dust-flecked, as was the black Stetson and faded dark blue trousers. The women he encountered in his wandering craft were often taken in by Charlie Siringo's finely chiseled mouth below the dark mustache and the smile in those piercing brown eyes.

His becoming a Pinkerton could be traced directly to the arrival of a noted phrenologist at Caldwell, Kansas, a cattle town on the border between Kansas and the Indian Territory. That the phrenologist chanced to be blind only added to his allure, and so it was that Charlie Siringo was one of those crowding into the Leland Hotel. At this time a man named Henry Brown had been city marshal, with Brown reluctantly agreeing to have the blind phrenologist examine the bony structure of his head, and to have Brown leave angrily upon hearing some unflattering remarks said against him. But Charlie Siringo knew what the phrenologist had just said was true, because he knew that Brown had been a member of Billy the Kid's outlaw gang down in the Panhandle of Texas, something Siringo had kept to himself. Later on he'd come to regret this, for after Siringo had left this neck of the woods came the news that Henry Brown and one of his deputies had in broad daylight held up the nearby Medicine Lodge Bank and killed the bank president and his cashier. As for Charlie Siringo, after considerable coaxing from his friends he'd let that blind phrenologist splay those long bony fingers over his skull, then to be told about a large stubborn bump which meant Siringo had a possible future as a newspaper editor or detective.

Thus Charlie Siringo's first stab at being a detective came when some Texas cattlemen asked him to track down cattle thieves infesting parts of western Texas and New Mexico. When this job panned out, twenty-four year old Charlie Siringo found himself in Chicago with his young wife and little baby. About this time the Haymarket riots broke out, with an anarchist's bomb killing and maiming over sixty of the city's police officers. Wanting nothing more than to track down those responsible for the bombing, Siringo presented himself at the offices of the famous Pinkerton Detective Agency. To his surprise he was hired on, and shortly afterward dispatched by train out to Denver. In the years to come Charlie Siringo was sent up to Alaska, British Columbia, and down to Old Mexico, though most of his work as a detective took place in the western states. Those years also saw Charlie Siringo separating from his wife, something he often regretted.

Though he'd grown fond of Denver, Siringo felt the rawboned western city was becoming too large and much to his sorrow a haven for a con clan headed up by the notorious Lou Blonger. Blonger, a French-Canadian who had migrated to the mining camps while still a youth, had become the king of the Denver underworld, and it was rumored that a secret line of communication ran from Blonger's saloon to the office of the city's chief of police.

"Let the city council fret over that," Charlie Siringo said quietly as he returned the curt nod of a man seated in a buggy. "Well, Bucknell, I see Captain Farley's got you running errands."

"Always the clever wit," came the man's surly response.

Tossing his valise into the back seat, Charlie Siringo hopped onto the leather seat as the buggy wheeled away from the curbing. He knew that Bucknell and the other field operatives working here at Denver resented his being able to work alone, and chiefly that Captain Mike Farley often singled him out for the tougher assignments. But unlike most of the other detectives, these being men brought in from eastern states, Charlie Siringo was more cowhand than detective, could find hardcases in almost trackless terrain, that Siringo knew his way around the mining towns of the west. He'd posed as both outlaw and miner, and every so often he would run into men knowing him under an assumed name. Many a time he'd charmed his way out of tight spots, along with romancing a woman or two.

"Look, Bucknell, for what it's worth," he said in that easy Texas drawl, "last year I asked Cap'n Farley to have you work with me."

A corner of Bucknell's mouth lifted in a thoughtful scowl. "That so?"

"Never got beyond the talking stage."

"Appreciate that, Charlie."

"Haven't been here in a month of Sundays!"

"So what's new?"

"You know as much as I do about why I'm here," muttered Charlie Siringo as one eye slid to a street corner and a couple of hard-eyed men idling there.

"The captain's been pretty tightlipped last couple of months. But I gather why you're here is because of the killings . . ."

The buggy swung around still another street corner, then to veer into morning shadows stretching along a large brick building. Tying up, Bucknell clambered out as the man he'd picked up at the train depot reached for his valise, to have Charlie Siringo pause when he saw the humoring glint in Bucknell's eyes.

Siringo said dryly, "Should have known I wouldn't be in town for any length of time." He shoved the valise back onto the seat and followed after Bucknell, crossing the sidewalk.

Charlie Siringo's last view of the man he worked for had been of Captain Mike Farley standing ramrod straight before one of the windows in his second floor office while staring out at the city peeling up the mountainside. When the summons to Bucknell's hesitant knock had brought them into the room, Siringo found the captain turning away from that very same window but clad now in shades of brown—suit, vest, tie, and the shirt a sort of yellowy white. Farley was more commonly known amongst his operatives as Iron Mike, but out of his rather acute hearing, and because of the iron gray hair shading the longish face. He was tall, around six-two, sparse of build but with an erect, military carriage. Farley reached for an old briar pipe resting on a bed of discarded ashes in an ashtray fashioned from the brass casing of a Hotchkiss shell. The aromatic stench of tobacco smoke pricked at their nostrils, and the words of Captain Farley punching at them like a round leaving the barrel of a Winchester.

"These killings have to stop!" There was a reproachful glance at Bucknell.

"Ah, excuse me," said Bucknell as he left.

Then a crooking finger brought Charlie Siringo after the captain pivoting to open another door. Farley marched down a long hallway, unlocked a door to enter a dark, smallish room. As he brought light to a lamp, Siringo closed the door. Now the flickering flames revealed a large map hanging from one wall and huddled close to the map several photographs and other hanging paperwork. Stepping closer, Siringo studied the faces of the men in the photographs before a word from the captain brought his eyes focused on the map.

"The latest killings have taken place down here at Plymouth in northern Texas. Three men gunned down at long range. All within a span of a week."

"Plymouth—not much down there but a lot of prairie and the Canadian River."

"And what people living around Plymouth refer to it as a free love colony."

"That's a new one on me, Captain."

A jabbing finger punctuated among the glossy photographs, and with Captain Farley saying, "Three of these men were Reb sharpshooters; the pair of others, Lyndall and Snider, Union soldiers. All of them have long since parted ways with the military."

"You're saying that one of them could be doing

these killings?"

"Perhaps. What I've discovered is that all of these men move around a lot. Snider, for instance, has just settled into Red Lodge, territorial Montana."

"Montana's a far piece from Texas."

"Not that far, Siringo." The captain's eyes lifted to a picture frame hanging above everything else attached to the wall. "There's our killer, Siringo."

Charlie Siringo frowned at the white backing behind the protective glass on the picture frame. "I get your drift, Captain."

"Yes, Siringo, I want the face of our killer framed up there." A hand reached to a small table. Picking up a large manila envelope held closed by encircling red string, he thrust it at Charlie Siringo. "This includes expense money and a railroad ticket. Well?"

"Sure enjoyed coming back to Denver," he said wryly, and fifteen minutes later Charlie Siringo found himself heaving out of the buggy in front of the train depot, and reaching back for his valise.

"Did you speak to the captain about me?"

He took one last look at Pinkerton operative Bucknell. "I didn't even have time to go to the bathroom. You know, a man deserves some time off."

"You could quit, Siringo."

"Could," he grinned. "Keep your fly buttoned up, Bucknell."

Three days later Detective Charlie Siringo stood looking at dust spurting out from behind a departing stagecoach. After a tired yawn he managed to take in a narrow main street hedged by frame buildings and a few people still braving a noon sun on this hot summery day in Plymouth, Texas.

Along the way he'd had ample time to study everything Captain Farley had crammed into that manila envelope. Included had been a smaller version of the map, which detailed that these killings had taken place from southern Texas clear up to Montana. This had left Charlie Siringo with the sobering realization that more than one man must be involved. Moving on, he didn't find the town marshal in his office but across the street at a saloon hunkered over a cold beer.

"Siringo, uh? You know, Siringo, Pinkertons aren't too welcome out thisaway."

"For a fact," said Charlie as he pulled a chair away from the table and sat down. "Mind if I spring for another beer?"

The town marshal shrugged indifferently and said, "Beer tastes the same never no mind who springs for it. Along with disliking Pinkertons, folks hereabouts don't care none a'tall for them homesteading out along the river."

"I suppose not," responded Siringo as the only barkeep plunked down a couple of cold glasses of beer to scoop up the silver dollar and leave a scowl behind. "Just what is this . . . free love colony . . ."

"Wife swapping and other sinnin' is what it's all about. Good riddance I say to them got gunned down."

"Did you check out what happened?"

"Nope," he said flatly. "Out of my territory."

"What about the sheriff?"

"Expect you'd better ask the sheriff, Siringo."

"Well, you've been most generous, marshal. Just where is this colony?"

"West along the river. But I'd ride in easily, I was you, Siringo."

"Oh, hell, Toby, you didn't have to tell him that."

Charlie Siringo slid his eyes to one of the eavesdroppers perched with others on a bench crowding the front wall. Then he rose and dug out another silver dollar, which he tossed at the barkeep along with a wide grin, and these parting words. "Buy my pallbearers a round."

Expecting that he would have paid a lot more for the rented horse had the hostler known of his connection to the Pinkerton Detective Agency, Charlie Siringo had merely stated he was a carpetbagger going out to hustle those at the free love colony out of their hard-earned dollars. Even so, the grimace stayed with Siringo until the green broke bronc stopped trying to get the kinks out of its back and settled into an easy canter. Though, by this time Charlie Siringo had broken out into a sweat. But it felt good to be back in Texas and on a horse again, even though the place where he was reared, Matagorda County, lay far to the south. Then all he'd known was being saddlebound with the ground for a bed and the sky for covering. He began rolling into shape, a contented cigarette.

A couple of hours later as he gauged by the sun, he spotted around five antelope in the hazy distance, these farther to the north. But westward the sight of rising dust brought him sitting taller in the saddle.

Cautiously he let the bronc lope on, until topping a rise, he came upon a large wagon heading his way, the back crammed with household goods, and on the front seat a woman and two children and a bearded man rigged out in sodbuster clothing sawing at the reins. Siringo rode on down.

His friendly wave was greeted with bared teeth by the sodbuster bringing up his rifle, and quickly Siringo drawled, "Easy, mister, I mean no harm."

"Then stand aside and let us pass."

Since the woman, somewhat comely and in her early thirties, had bold eyes, he figured these folks were part of that free love colony. "One question," Siringo said curtly. "I was summoned here by R. J. Rafferty."

"That was no question, mister."

"We know him," the woman said, with the tip of her tongue flicking suggestively against her lips. "Back there, about five miles, is the settlement."

"Obliged," said Siringo, and reining sharply to get his horse out of the way of the wagon bolting on. He held while staring after the wagon lumbering eastward. "Saucy wench. But maybe a touch of the Black Widow in her."

On a day such as this Charlie Siringo figured there wouldn't be any chimney smoke to guide him in, but less than three miles farther on he sighted in on a scattering of log buildings. He took in the fluttering rows of corn in a field close by the tree-guarded river, and others of wheat and what he took to be barley. Then he reined up so abruptly the bronc took to rearing up.

"Easy," he muttered anxiously, as in him came this

feeling he was being watched, and most probably by men sighting down long rifle barrels.

The gist of the report in the papers given him by Captain Mike Farley told of three men belonging to this settlement being bushwhacked. And from long range. Included also was a copy of the letter from a gent named Rafferty, who Siringo surmised, must be the big chief out here. Sucking simmering afternoon air into his lungs, Siringo shouted, "I was summoned here by R. J. Rafferty. Name's Siringo—from the Pinkerton Detective Agency out of Denver. So I'm coming in with my hands held high"—and in a lower and worried monotone—"and with this Texas son shaking in his boots. Don't comfort me none either these sodbusters can't shoot all that good."

Siringo had walked his horse onward about a quarter of a mile, when suddenly two riders burst out of the cornfield. They were carbon copies of the sodbuster he'd encountered earlier, big, burly men with floppy black hats and suspenders straining at wide shoulders, and to Siringo's amused eyes astride plow horses.

While one of the riders held back but kept his rifle glued to his shoulder, the other came in to yank the rifle out of Siringo's saddle boot, and say blusteringly.

"Your handgun, Siringo."

Through a grimace he said, "Why, since you know I'm Charlie Siringo?"

"Because you speak like a Texan."

"Can't argue against that." Bringing down a nervous hand, he lifted his coat aside, and quickly the sodbuster grabbed the Colt .45.

Hemming in Charlie Siringo like cowhands sidling to either side of a longhorn wanting to bolt, they loped toward the settlement along a vague trail. By the time they were in amongst the buildings, a crowd was gathering. They brought Siringo over to what appeared to be a meeting hall or perhaps a store, since the building was larger than the others and had a covered front porch, and to Siringo's surprise glass in the two windows out of which peered others belonging to this free love settlement. Now through the open door stepped a man, who promptly removed his hat and used the red handkerchief he was holding to swipe at his bald pate and then wipe along his shirt collar. He was smaller and somewhat older than most clustering in, but his eyes told Charlie Siringo all he needed to know.

"Mr. Rafferty, glad to see you."

"Perhaps," he replied soberly. "You are from the Pinkertons?"

"Yup—been doing detective work for some time now."

"Well, if you aren't, we'll find out. Please, get off that horse and come join me where it's cooler. Tend to his horse, Jason."

"What about his gun?"

"Please return it to . . ."

"Charlie Siringo . . . and obliged." Though he felt a little better when the Colt was nestling in his holster, he didn't start shedding some of that nervous feeling until he'd settled across from R. J. Rafferty at an oaken table. He had a quick smile for a woman bringing over a pot of coffee and two cups, then shortly afterward a word from his host sent everyone scurrying outside.

"All I can say, Mr. Siringo, is that we will not be driven out of here."

"You mean these killings will go on if you don't skedaddle?"

"We don't know that. But we suspect these killings were done by order of a rancher or ranchers, townspeople, those opposed to our way of life."

"There is a pattern here."

"I don't understand?"

"Let's mosey outside."

Out away from the front porch, Charlie Siringo asked where the killings had taken place, to be told that those gunned down had been working out in the fields, and under the curious eyes of the settlement he trudged alongside R. J. Rafferty, but all the while Siringo took in the open lay of the land fringing away from the river. He asked one question, to which Rafferty said, "No, Mr. Siringo, whoever did the killings stayed well away from the river. Afterward, in every instance, our men scoured along the river banks. They found no tracks, of men nor horse, though there were old hoof markings made by both horses and cattle. We searched all of the fields; found nothing to indicate the killer had been in there."

Since the settlement lay on the north side of the river, Charlie Siringo disregarded land flowing in from the south. Northward, beyond the short fringe of cropland, lay nothing but open land, shimmering now in the afternoon haze. But there were a few outcroppings, these at a distance of a mile or more. His mind checked this out, and the butte located just beyond.

"A man would be working in the field." There was a vague sweep of the man's arm. "Suddenly he would fall."

"There was no sound of a rifle?"

"Later . . . later there would come a sharp report like thunder . . . distantly."

"Meaning the man who died never heard anything . . . just the agonizing realization he'd been shot . . . then to perish quickly."

"The first man who was killed—we found his body about an hour later. The mule was still standing there hitched to the plow. His wife, it was she who found Sam Delaney. Found him, Mr. Siringo, with a gaping hole in his chest . . . a . . . a bigger one in his back where the slug had passed through."

He looked away from the bitter agony playing across R. J. Rafferty's sun-scoured face and to the north, and quietly he said, "As I stated before, sir, this fits a pattern."

Rafferty turned to move slowly with the Pinkerton operative back toward the buildings.

"We believe that perhaps one or more men have been doing these killings. What has happened here, Mr. Rafferty, fits the same pattern of killings in other areas. We're speaking of hired assassins . . . sharpshooters, if you please." Pausing, Siringo nodded northerly. "He was out there someplace, perhaps one man with a long-range weapon. Coming in quietly; leaving just as silently. I'll get my horse and scout this out."

"It must be as you say. We are not riflemen, Mr. Siringo." His pondering eyes scanned the distant rises. "Such a long way. What manner of man has the eye of an eagle?"

"Used a telescopic sight," came Siringo's dry reply.

After his horse was brought over, Charlie Siringo loped out under the anxious eyes of R. J. Rafferty and some holding rifles. He struck out due north away from the settlement over fairly level ground. Along the way, he checked out possible hiding places. Long years of holding to a horse and being around guns told him he was about a mile out, that close at hand were higher elevations giving a rifleman an open view of the fields stretching away from the river and on this side of the buildings.

Now he rode up one of the rocky elevations, looked about carefully for any disturbed ground or empty shell casings. He came down to prairieland and up another gentle slope, and it was here that a satisfied glimmer beamed out of his eyes. For back of the rise a gully cut northeasterly; the escape route of the bushwhacker. Dismounting, he tied the reins to a mesquite bush. He went on, carefully, worked his way around more shrubbery and scattered rock until his eyes landed on a stretch of the rise containing large flat rocks, and then he knew, and Siringo murmured, "Just under a mile to them fields. About the right distance for a turkey shoot. Still, a man's got to be awful damned good at this range."

Scanning the ground around the flat rocks, he soon realized the ground had been swept clean, possibly by someone using shrubbery. His search for discarded shell casings proved fruitless, or of any tracks left by the ambusher. But he would bet his best Sunday hat that the killer had worked his way back to his horse tethered below in that gully and cut out. By now it would be a dry trail, since Charlie Siringo was certain the ambusher was a long way away and out of Texas.

When Siringo returned to the settlement, it was to have everyone congregate in the meeting hall, and this included the yonkers. He brought out the photographs given him by Captain Farley.

"Folks, these men could have passed through here. Or there's every possibility you might have seen one of them over at Plymouth."

"Damned right I want to catch that killer!"

"Not according to Rafferty out at that free love colony."

"Look, Siringo, every ablebodied man and half the women in Potter County have reasons to hate what's going on out there."

"Expect you're right, sheriff. I tried showing these pictures I'm carrying around town . . . but folks are sure tightlipped."

"Sometimes they can get a little testy."

Charlie Siringo pushed up from the chair to say, "Nobody out at that settlement recognized any of these men." Reaching to the desk, he shoved the photographs into the manila envelope. "You will keep me informed if you come across anything . . ."

"Yup, can do that, Siringo. You heading out?"

"I've felt more comfortable in a lot of other places. But if I stick around somebody just might take a liking to me . . . just maybe pick out one of these men as being the killer."

"Could be," grinned the sheriff. "About equal to our chances of getting a gully washer today, or this year for that matter."

Around midafternoons he'd gotten into the habit of having a cup or two of Arbuckles washed down with a handrolled. But now upon leaving the sheriff's office, Siringo took that long stroll back to his hotel. The sound of the lobby door thudding shut behind him was echoed by the day clerk thrusting a yellow envelope toward Charlie Siringo as he said, "Just got delivered, Mr. Siringo."

He shoved a dime into the clerk's hand still hanging suggestively over the counter and found the staircase. His room, an enclosure of faded blue wallpaper mildewed with age, lay in shadow. So he pulled aside the curtain on the west window and tore the envelope open. The telegram bore Captain Farley's unmistakable terse prose.

KILLING WITH SAME MODUS OF OPERATION HAPPENED TWO DAYS AGO AT RUSSELL SPRINGS, KANSAS. PROCEED THERE IMMEDIATELY.

CAPTAIN M. FARLEY.

"Russell Springs? I do recollect it's west . . . along the Smoky Hill River. And something else?"

Siringo pulled out of the manila envelope the photographs, discarded all of them but one.

"Could you be our killer?" He studied a face that he figured had adorned some wanted posters. The man had swarthy skin and a pinched sort of gleam in his eyes, the mouth a sullen line in a thick blue-tinted beard. The name on the back as scrawled in

Captain Farley's elaborate scrawl said, Cyril Lyndall, that he'd served with Sheridan's western army as a sharpshooter. There was also Lyndall's last known address—the town of Modoc, just west of Scott City.

"Shouldn't be all that hard tracking him down. After that I'm cutting out for some trout fishing in the Colorado Rockies."

And once Charlie Siringo had clambered into a stagecoach the following morning, he never looked back at Plymouth awakening to the sound of rain spilling out of a sullen gray sky.

"Hope it gully washes that town away."

Chapter Three

The bugling call of an antelope carved a hole through mist blanketing along bottomland. This provoked from Joshua Tremane a grimacing smile, and from the Russian elkhound on whose shoulders his big bony hand was draped, an eager growl. His other hand lay limp and trembling on the padded arm of the chair. The coffee had chilled in the cup on the side table as had the whitish gravy humped over sourdough biscuits, for this morning there was more pain than usual, pain that told him of the crippling disease ravaging at his large frame, reminded him also that he no longer controlled his destiny.

The eyes of Joshua Tremane, cattle baron and philanthropist, revealed everything, the bitter anger, deep well of despair, and that arrogant glimmer. For he was not a man who gave up easily. Nor forgave others their trespasses against him. Which is why in the broad reaches of the Madison Valley he had few close friends. He was set in his ways, garrulous, domineering.

Once the charcoal suit showed to good advantage

Tremane's tallish frame, but now it was merely folds of broadloom draped over wasting muscles and protruding bone. He was as an oak tree besieged by some parasitic malignancy. The cheeks of his broad face had saucered in, the weathered skin had paled, the full head of graying hair a wild mane touching upon thinning shoulders. He had denied himself the vanity of a beard, or perhaps it was because this would hide the stubborn thrust to his wide jaw, the churlish mouth. He was also a man who brooked no disobedience from either his segundo or thirty-odd hands working out here at his Double Tree ranch.

Now his thoughts lifted beyond the front porch of his ranchhouse to a shaft of fiery red knifing in between distant peaks to the east. What he viewed from where he sat was scattered timber following the upthrusting valley wall to foothills ridging onto the Madison Range. In the hazy distance he could make out a small bunch of antelope and familiar rock formations serving to mark the eastern borders of his ranch. Below this curled the river, the Madison, which rose in that Yellowstone country east of the mountains and flowed northward to unite with the Jefferson and Gallatin at Three Forks to form the Missouri River. But for the mist clouding along the river Joshua Tremane could have glimpsed trout springing up in search of their morning meal, and but for his damnable illness the rancher would be out their trying his hand at flycasting.

"Prince," he muttered in a low rumbling voice to his dog, "have I sinned all that much?"

But the sins of Joshua Tremane were many, even though he considered his past misdeeds merely ploys to gain control of this vast ranch holding sway over much of the valley. Back more years than he cared to remember he'd left Philadelphia, thirtyish and with a considerable inheritance. At first his intentions were to settle in around Billings, and he had purchased a few modest sections of ranchland. Later on during hunting trips into this region of territorial Montana, Joshua Tremane had settled his eyes upon this valley. Shortly thereafter he sold out his other holdings and came here. Though a lot of ranchland was taken up, he gained a foothold, then a few bad winters caused others to sell out and leave. There were others who managed to hang on. But over the years he whittled away at them, with money, veiled threats, and in a few cases, with violence.

To those sodbusters daring enough to file claims along the river, his Double Tree waddies were an unrelenting scourge. By Joshua Tremane's order they were either burned out or given a certain time to load up their meager belongings. Only the foolhardy resisted, and it was now that a bitter scowl etched itself across Joshua Tremane's passive face.

"Bellcone was too damned stubborn."

His thoughts centered upon John Bellcone, and all of the trouble the sodbuster had given him, this as spokesman for others crowding in along the river. Bellcone had spurned all of his offers. Only then did Joshua Tremane order his men to kill the sodbuster's livestock and burn the small fields of wheat and oats, along with dealing out the same brand of punishment to the others. The first casualty was John Bellcone's oldest son, who'd been brazen enough to take out after the Double Tree hands armed only with a cap and ball rifle. The Bellcone kid was the first to be buried just west of the river. And then came the lightning storm which kept Joshua Tremane overnighting in Ennis. Just on the verge of turning in, he'd been crossing the lobby of the Fremont Hotel to head upstairs when the front door opened and his foreman put in a hasty appearance.

"One of those Bellcone kids is in town."

Joshua Tremane paused with one hand reaching for the bannister as he swung to look back at Ozzie Browning. The rancher was tired, having been closeted with his banker and lawyer for the better part of the day. He had decided against suppering here at the hotel, and since he was neither a drinking man nor gambled, this storm would keep him overnight, though it was the rancher's habit to get up at a late hour for a light repast.

He said gruffly, "Strange that he'd be alone?"

"That kid is looking for a doctor, Mr. Tremane. From what I overheard his folks have come down with smallpox."

His face settling into pondering lines, Joshua Tremane glanced over at the desk clerk straining to hear what was being said, with a jerk of his head bringing his foreman following down a back hallway and to the open back door. Here he turned to face Browning, and to say quietly, "This town has two doctors. One of them, Mitchell, went up to Bozeman. That leaves Doc Kreuger. Now here's what you're to do."

During the last few weeks what the rancher had ordered his foreman to do back at Ennis brought moments of regret. What happened was that Ozzie Browning and a couple of other Double Tree hands had the doctor ride with them out to the ranch, Browning's bald lie being that one of his men had busted his leg after being thrown by a bronc. Shortly afterward, word was brought out to Joshua Tremane that John Bellcone and his wife had succumbed to smallpox. Maybe they wouldn't have pulled through this had the doctor made it out there, Tremane had often mused. There was this voice that kept telling Joshua Tremane he'd committed murder.

"Then . . . then Melissa had to start seeing this . . . this Danny Bellcone . . ."

The woman in question was Tremane's only kin, his daughter, Melissa Tremane, just turned nineteen. The trouble had started last summer when he'd let Melissa stay in Ennis as a guest of the Hendleys. Only when autumn was touching upon the valley did word reach the rancher that Danny Bellcone had set his hat for Melissa. Tremane's response was swift, first in packing his daughter off to that eastern college, and a few days later some of his men cornered Bellcone in an Ennis saloon. They didn't use guns but their rockhard fists and boots upon Danny Bellcone, and with a warning that he was to stay clear of Joshua Tremane's daughter.

"Now . . . she's coming home . . ." The rancher's eyes widened into a pleased smile, which also served to chase away some of his pain. "This afternoon."

"Joshua?"

"Uh . . . oh, you're here already . . ."

The dog came around the chair and somewhat grudgingly let Sid Mason brush a workworn hand along its neck, but with a low growl rumbling out of its mouth. The Double Tree hands gave the ranchhouse and the elkhound a wide berth. Oftentimes it would take out after a lone steer or try to chase away grazing horses, and it would kill any dogs that wandered onto the place, and coyotes. More than one waddy had remarked that the elkhound mirrored the aloofness of its owner. Even the cook, a former cowhand named Art Weaver, stepped gingerly when the dog, Prince, came around for its daily meals out back of the house. Strangely enough the elkhound never bothered chasing after any of the cats, though Weaver felt the dog would get around to them in time. As for Sid Mason, he had hired on at the Double Tree back when it was just a scrambling of buildings, this when the Indians were still out raiding and before gold was discovered up in the Tobacco Roots. He wasn't all that tall but had a commanding presence, and had been Tremane's first segundo. Passing into his fifties had turned Mason into a dried-out hulk of the man he had once been, had silvered his hair and tightened the weathered skin on his bony face. He knew better than anyone the moods of Joshua Tremane, was privy to all that Tremane had done in the making of this ranch.

"Easy now," he said upon letting go of the rancher's arm and reaching for the crutches.

The padded ends of the crutches under his arms, the steadying hand of Mason upon his shoulder, Joshua Tremane said hoarsely, "If I don't attend church the ways of the evil one shall surely come upon me."

Sid Mason knew this was a dry attempt at humor by the rancher, and he replied with a wry grin wedging at his mouth, "You still fixin' on deliverin' this morning's sermon?"

Every so often Joshua Tremane would preach from the pulpit of the church he'd help put up in Ennis. Through the years his monthly tithes were larger than most of the fifty or so other parishioners, while his voice was often heeded in other church matters. It hadn't always been this way, but the passage of years had mellowed the bitter talk against him. That he was the controlling stockholder in the local bank also had a lot to do with Joshua Tremane gaining a certain respectability. However there were a few still carrying a lot of hatred for the Double Tree.

The rancher managed to hobble down the few stone steps and be helped into the large carriage by Sid Mason, where he sank back upon the thick leather cushions of the rear seat. He let the hated crutches drop at his feet, then Tremane snugged the woolen blanket around his legs and over his lap to keep the morning chill away, though before too long it would probably warm into the seventies again. As the carriage rolled away from the house and found the northward-running lane, Tremane reached over and picked up the leather-clad bible, but didn't open it as pain spasmed through his chest. Inwardly he cursed it away; despite his abstinence from liquor, swearing was part and parcel of Joshua Tremane.

"Might rain later today," Mason remarked as he whipped the matched team of grays into a canter.

"Appears that way."

"It'll sure be nice to have Melissa around again."

There was no response from Joshua Tremane.

He glanced over his shoulder at the rancher huddled over the bible. There's going to be trouble, pondered Sid Mason, unless that Bellcone kid has enough sense to stay clear of Ennis. It would be like Melissa Tremane to write back and tell her friends in town she was coming home. The trouble as he saw it was her taking up with Bellcone again. Maybe the hands should have used their guns instead of fists.

"Trouble," mused Sid Mason, "haven't had any of that for a spell. But I've got this bad feeling that things are gonna change mighty quick."

The lane they were on was one of many hubbing toward Ennis, the only cowtown in the valley. Although farther to the north a little under ten miles, lay the settlement of Tanner's Corner. Ahead of them and just pushing in through the outlying buildings was another buggy, which Sid Mason figured held more folks going to church. He didn't consider himself much of a religious person, as he liked his nights on the town, but driving the man he worked for in here every Sunday had gotten to be habit-forming. Some of the saloons would be open, and a mercantile store or two, and Sid Mason's rheumy-blue eyes narrowed worriedly when he swung onto the long main drag of Ennis spilling to the north and spotted some freighters idling under the covered arcade fronting the Moonlight Tavern.

"We're here," he called back softly.

"I'm well aware of that, Sid." Joshua Tremane snapped the bible shut and began surveying the passing buildings.

Up on the front seat, Sid Mason switched the reins to his left hand and brushed his coat aside. For he'd just recognized those muleskinners as working for that Bellcone kid. While they had picked it up right away that the big, fancy carriage belonged to Joshua Tremane, as one of them now shouldered away from a support pole and hurried into the saloon, to have Sid Mason utter bitterly, "Should have taken a side street."

There was still time for Mason to swing the carriage onto a side street. This notion struck him, as did the cold fact be wasn't about to dodge trouble, which he knew was coming when the man Joshua Tremane hated stepped out of the saloon. There was Danny Bellcone and four others, and when Sid Mason brought the carriage abreast of the saloon, it was to have Bellcone step out into the street. Only then did Joshua Tremane realize something was wrong, and only then did he sight in on Bellcone.

"You damned fool, I told you to stay clear of this town!"

"No man tells me what to do! Especially someone who had me stomped half to death."

Mason let his sixgun drop back into the holster when he realized that Danny Bellcone was unarmed. But what worried him was the way the others were crowding out into the street and fanning out, and that Danny Bellcone had been drinking. Would they attack a man crippled as Tremane was at the moment? He brought his attention back to Bellcone, took in quickly the wavy head of brownish hair under the worn hat and the handsome features, the lithe frame encased in rough clothing, could see how Melissa Tremane would fall for Bellcone. But if Joshua Tremane hated scum such as this, that was good enough for Sid Mason, although unlike the man he worked for, in him was more of a forgiving nature.

"Let it be, Danny," he said quickly, nervously, "call off your friends."

"Reckoned you'd be coming in today, Mr. Tremane," he said derisively, with a quick smile that included Sid Mason. Stepping closer, Bellcone placed a hand on the carriage door. "There was no need for you to send your men after me. 'Cause it was your daughter who chased after me."

"Why . . . you damned pup . . . I'll . . ."

"What, hit me with one of your crutches." His face hardening, Danny Bellcone added, "She's due in today, I hear, your daughter, Tremane. But that don't mean nothing to me. What I'm saying, Tremane, is that I aim to stay clear of her. Just make sure she does the same."

"Mason, clear the hell out of here!" yelled Joshua Tremane, a man so blinded by anger and hatred and contempt at the moment that he hadn't realized the carriage was pulling upstreet. Damn those Bellcones! To be publicly humiliated like this! He's lying! He'll try to see Melissa.

Sid Mason brought the carriage onto an angling street curling away from the river. Then he walked the horses past other buggies and carriages to pull up by the side door of Grace Episcopal Church, a steepled building set on a gentle hillock around which grew sheltering oaks. A slight breeze swept against Mason's face as he tied up the reins. Swinging down, he stepped back and said, "They were liquored up, Joshua, just letting off some steam."

"We'll discuss it later," replied Tremane, and with angry hands he picked up the crutches and thrust them out at Sid Mason. Tremane got out stiffly, but with his eyes still filled with the resentment of what had happened. He must not, he told himself, carry this hatred into the house of the Living God. These people he would soon be preaching to deserved more than the retorts of an angry man. Later there would be plenty of time to deal properly with Bellcone and his drunken cronies.

Hobbling into the side entryway with the help of the only man he trusted, Joshua Tremane had a smile for one of the deacons, shoemaker Jens Pederson, who said piously, "I can't tell you, Mr. Tremane, how much we are looking forward to your sermon for today."

"Yes," came Tremane's curt reply, "I do appreciate that. How is Pastor Lindholm?"

"Coming along slowly, I'm afraid. But we hope and pray he'll be well enough to preach next Sunday. But today our prayers go out to you."

Moving up onto the altar, Tremane settled into a chair with the help of his crutches, laid them aside, and was handed his bible by Mason, who went down into the nave and sat down in one of the pews. Sunlight pierced through the multi-glassed windows, which were purchased by Joshua Tremane on one of his many trips to Salt Lake City. Up in the choir loft a mixed choir of men and women held up their hymnals at the final pealing of the church bell. The deacon, Pederson, rose from a side chair and went to stand behind the pulpit. His opening messages went quickly, and at his silent nod, the choir and those seated below burst into song.

Seated in the clerestory, Joshua Tremane felt his anger subsiding. He also felt that certain weakness pricking at him, the occasional rasp of pain knifing through his thinning frame. Sometime later his name was called out, and Tremane rose with the help of the altar railing. He shuffled over to ease onto a high stool placed for him behind the pulpit. Opening the bible, he gazed out at the expectant faces of people he'd known a long time. What they viewed was the ravaged face of Joshua Tremane, the unyielding eyes under the thick and shaggy brows. Most of the parishioners owed money to the local bank, and thus an uneasy fealty to rancher Tremane. They felt a lot easier since good times had come to the valley in the form of miners passing through on their way up to Virginia City or Nevada City or the diggings lower on the spiny ridge of the Tobacco Roots. They'd known the hard underside of the coin too, of lean years when many of the locals, businessmen and ranchers alike, couldn't make their loan payments and were forced out. So they listened with an edging of respect as the rancher spoke in acid tones from the book of Proverbs.

". . . So my fellow Christians . . . I say onto you . . . the fear of the Lord is to hate evil . . . pride and arrogance . . . and the evil way . . . and the forward mouth, do I hate . . ."

Joshua Tremane's arms lifted to include those seated before him as once again his deep baritone voice battened against the closed windows.

"For today . . . this very morning I was beset upon by evil men. Men who squander their money in the saloons of this town. Drinking on the Sabbath is an abomination. But I come here today not to condemn from this pulpit . . . from this house of the Living God . . . nor to judge the way of the sluggard . . ."

Without warning one of the high side windows exploded inward, strewing shards of colored glass onto many of those seated in the long pews, with a large rock thudding against a man's upper neck and face, and with a woman screaming her sudden fear. A rock came through another window to have those seated in the pews duck out of the way. While up on the pulpit Joshua Tremane shouted, "It's Bellcone . . . those damned muleskinners!"

Lurching to his feet, Sid Mason, as did a few other men, broke for the side door and spilled outside. All they glimpsed was tall grass springing back into place past the sheltering trees along with spotting some hats bobbing away.

"How could they?"

"Just who the hell would do such a thing?"

"I ain't speculating none on that," murmured Sid Mason, though it was clear in his thoughts that Danny Bellcone was behind this. "There's a lot of strangers in town . . . and a lot of corn whiskey being gulleted down today."

"This is blasphemy."

"That it be, deacon," agreed Sid Mason.

"Well, is anybody going after them?"

"By now they'll be hiding out in some saloon. Best we let the sheriff handle this."

"That is, if you can get Ben Taylor away from that pinochle game."

* * *

Coming around a long bend in the Bozeman to Ennis road, the stagecoach driver sawed back on the reins and expelled a few choice words for the carriage blocking his way. "Some danged fool?"

"That fool," Old Anse Pickard informed the driver sharing the high seat of the Resse & Colmar stagecoach, "is none other than Tremane of the Double Tree. Still, a helluva spot to pick up his daughter."

"Don't cut no mustard with me who he is, Anse. Now, whoa, ease up now." He managed to halt his span of horses, and afterward to stare disdainfully at Old Anse Pickard climbing down and began jawing with Sid Mason.

"Town's barely a mile away, Sid."

"Not my idea." He stepped over and smiled up at Melissa Tremane hopping down from the stagecoach. "Have a good trip?"

"A long one, Sid. Is something wrong?"

"Your pa . . . Joshua's idea. That your luggage up there?"

"I'll hand it down," said the driver.

When Melissa Tremane got into the carriage, it was to gaze upon the troubled face of her father. But knowing of his many moods, there was merely a kiss and an exchange of pleasantries as their carriage swung back toward Ennis shimmering under an early afternoon sun. Only when Sid Mason brought their carriage onto a lane that would bring them around the town snugged along the river did her inquiring eyes go to her father again.

"There has been a little trouble," he began.

What Melissa didn't to want tell her father at the

moment was that word had come to her of how some of the Double Tree hands had ganged up on Danny Bellcone. In a way she had expected something of this nature to happen, because it was common knowledge of the bad feelings which had existed between her father and the Bellcones, sodbusting at that time along the Madison River. Though slender and possessed with luminous hazel eyes, chestnut hair that spilled below her shoulders, a lot of her friends said Melissa Tremane had her father's temper and way with words. Oftentimes she'd thought of the scolding she would give her father for what he'd done to Danny Bellcone. Seeing him now, thinned out like this, the sickly tint to his skin, made her realize Joshua Tremane was dying. As for Danny Bellcone, there'd been plenty of time to try and forget about how she felt about him while back east at college. There'd been a few casual dates, and a couple of fine young men had asked for her hand in marriage. Laughingly she'd parried their offers, for always in her mind, despite her efforts to the contrary, was the sure knowledge she'd fallen in love with Danny. But, much to her dismay, Danny Bellcone had different feelings toward her.

"Daddy, I'm no longer a child. Did this trouble involve Danny Bellcone?"

Chillingly Joshua Tremane recited to his daughter about the encounter in Ennis, and of how Bellcone and those others had broken the church windows. "So under the circumstances I want you back at the ranch."

"Danny . . . breaking windows at the church . . ."

"Forget about him," Tremane said acidly, and then

inhaled sharply as he fought off the ebbing pain.

The thoughts of Sid Mason were also on what had happened on this Sabbath Day. But mostly on what Joshua Tremane had told him while they waited out the arrival of the stagecoach. "Joshua and me have gone up to Bozeman," he voiced silently, "Lord knows how many times. Him wanting to go up there so suddenlike just don't set well."

Seven years ago? Yup, pondered Sid Mason, it was about that time we made a trip to Bozeman, and with Joshua heading off to some saloon, place he'd never been before. Course, I tagged along. Struck some kind of deal with that saloon owner, as I recall. Weren't too long after that two men running shirt-tail outfits in the Madison Valley were gunned down under peculiar circumstances." He further recalled that nobody was made to answer for those killings.

Rubbing a worried hand along his jawline, Sid Mason mused inwardly, "Maybe if I rode into town and had a talk with Danny Bellcone. Then maybe again Joshua wanting to head for Bozeman is purely ranch business. Hope so. But this disease has turned him mean . . . killing mean. Guess it ain't all to do with Bellcone either. Reckon, too, it's Joshua knowing his time is runnin' out . . . and no one but Melissa to take over the Double Tree."

He whipped the horses into a faster gait, knowing that when they got back to the home ranch he'd have words with Joshua Tremane. In the past Joshua had heeded his counsel. While Sid Mason's fear now was that mere words would be the same as trying to plant wheat out on this rugged stretch of valley floor, the wind to shrivel it up, along with the wheat dying from lack of rainwater. That was Joshua, a man drawing all that hatred and bitterness inside, a hatred that tore a man apart same as if he had cancer.

"But I've got to try talking to Joshua. If nothing else, for Melissa's sake . . . and for all me and Joshua Tremane have been through together." He lashed out again with his whip. "Get a'goin a little faster . . . damnit."

Chapter Four

"It's a shame what you did to them eggs, Emma."

"Ben D. Taylor, you may be county sheriff, and wear that tinny little badge, but don't you come in here and tell me I can't fry eggs!"

"Ben's got her going again," remarked one of those occupying a table in the Old Tyme cafe.

A big, amiable man, Sheriff Taylor kept sad eyes fixed on the plate on his table. Poking at one of the eggs, a sad expression creasing down his eyes, he drawled, "Looks like a blacksmith fried this one; see how black the underside is, Emma. Now, mind you, I'm not complainin' none . . ."

"Then what do you call it?"

"Just offering some friendly advice is all."

"What, you big ugly hunk of . . ."

"I'll eat the eggs, Emma, I'll eat the eggs. Just don't be handling that butcher knife thataway. Just worried about my ulcers is all. Jens, pass over that pepper shaker."

"Now can we get back to the business at hand, sheriff," Jens Pederson said testily.

"That business being Danny Bellcone." Ben Taylor let his eyes drift around at the two other men clustered around the table, that being Abel Winger, a member of the town council, and to his left, the mayor of Ennis, C.T. Petrie. They'd been discussing somewhat vehemently what had happened yesterday morning at the Grace Episcopal Church, with Taylor responding with a nod or quiet word. He wasn't a man to be pushed around, and though the others knew this, it was plain to Ben Taylor that they were really voicing the feelings of Joshua Tremane.

"We should have kept Ed Delong on as town marshal."

"At least Ed would have done something by now."

"Gents, since Ed is now unemployed, this means you're stuck with Ben D. Taylor. Need I remind you again that I was duly elected by the people of this county. As a matter of fact, gents, Danny Bellcone even voted for me during the last election."

"Can't believe that . . . kid is of legal age."

"Which means he's damn well responsible for what happened yesterday at the church."

"Now that's a rather harsh word for a deacon."

Mayor Petrie said quickly, "Enough of this hassling over who or who not is guilty for breaking those windows. The point of fact, sheriff, is that Bellcone and his friends had words with Mr. Tremane yesterday morning. And we all know there's bad blood between them . . . over what happened . . ."

"Yup," agreed Taylor, "over Danny gettin beat to

hell by Tremane's bullyboys. I'd say Tremane earned any hard words thrown at him. But"—he set his coffee cup down hard—"I have to agree with you gents that Bellcone was one of those doin' the damage over at the church." Shoving his chair back, Taylor rose to tower over the table, that familiar grin chasing away how he felt about being cornered like this, on a Monday morning, with locals packing the cafe, and amongst them a few sharp-eared gossip hounds.

"Look, Ben," the mayor said by way of apology, "I'll spring for your breakfast."

"Hell's fire," cried out Emma, the shortorder cook, "let that old fart of a sheriff pay for his own vittles—burned eggs my foot."

Out on the boardwalk, Sheriff Ben Taylor ambled on until he could no longer be seen through the wide plate-glass windows, to pause and pull out a fat cigar from a checkered shirt pocket. Scratching a wooden match against his belt buckle, he let go with a satisfied belch before lighting the cigar, this even as he took in what was happening along main street. He was a week past his forty-first birthday, had been sheriff for more years than he cared to think about.

"Some broken windows are the least of my problems," he mused. At least once a night there'd be a ruckus at one of the saloons. Sometimes business places were broken into, while Ennis had become a prime stopping place for bunco artists and pickpockets, all because of the gold strikes. Anyone coming in had a hard time getting a room, prices had gone up considerable, even for those living here. He figured Virginia City and the other mining camps were boom and bust towns, that when the gold petered out he would enjoy sheriffing again.

At the western end of Beacon Street, Sheriff Ben Taylor took in the many freight wagons being loaded by a side dock of the Hoaglund Freighting Co. He knew some of the dock hands, but mostly they were new to town. A lot of them would work here for a week or two, then use their earnings to buy some mining equipment and head up to Virginia City. Up in the mountains, which were infested with highwaymen, most of them would go busted after a while, or have what gold they wrested from the diggings stolen when they were held up, and some would be killed. Rumors had floated down that the law up there, Sheriff Henry Plummer, had murderers and known thieves as his deputies. Another story going around was of a vigilante committee being formed up there. Earlier on, he'd even considered shucking his lawman's badge and heading for the diggings. But Ben Taylor hadn't, since good jobs were hard to find, and the truth of it was that he enjoyed his role as sheriff of Madison County. Though even before gold was discovered and the stampede to the Tobacco Roots started he had to face up to other problems. Most of these involved the ranchers trying to force out sodbusters, those trying to bring in woolies, and a few renegade Indians. What the valley had found after all the dust had settled was Joshua Tremane coming out the big winner.

Slowly, steadily, like molten lava streaming out of a volcano, the owner of the Double Tree had, in Ben Taylor's estimation, taken dominance over what happened in Ennis and a good part of the valley. A lot of folks had knuckled under to Tremane, but he hadn't, and never would. He prided himself on still having his self-respect, the fact he could look any man in the eye with a clear, untroubled gaze. Something that Joshua Tremane couldn't do, not so much as the man had used his money and a long rope and running iron, as had a lot of other ranchers. First of all, there were the Bellcones dying out at their place. What Ben Taylor had pieced together were more than suspicions of how Tremane had kept a doctor from heading out there. Not that Tremane wanted John Bellcone's meager hunk of land down along the Madison. But all because Melissa Tremane had decided she liked the tight fit to Danny Bellcone's worn levis. For a while the talk of Ennis had been her chasing after him, and with her sudden departure for that eastern college, the heavy hand of Joshua Tremane descending upon Bellcone. But before this, and here it got kind of grisly in the sheriff's opinion, the gunning down of Stephens and Riley Brown, ranchers and men he'd come to admire for how they were hacking out a living where others had simply given up. After both bodies were brought in, an autopsy performed by Doc Kreuger had produced leaden slugs equal in size and weight.

"Fifty caliber slugs," he murmured. Only those hunting grizzly bear up in the mountains or buffalo hunters carried a weapon capable of holding that particular caliber. At the time, around seven years ago, he knew for a cold fact nobody in the valley packed or even owned a .50 caliber rifle. Which to Ben Taylor meant someone had been paid to slip into the valley and do the killings. Another painful remembrance of about this time was the unexpected death of his wife, Lucille. She had borne him no children, but he still thought about her, would oftentimes go out to the cemetery and tend to her grave.

"As for Tremane," he went on silently, "shortly after the killings he gobbled up those ranches. As others had tried to do. Only he had more money . . . and I suspect, knew exactly what the others had bid so's to make his a little higher." Well, just more suspicions to go on.

Upon clearing the main storage building, Sheriff Taylor approached the stable area, where muleskinners were throwing harnesses onto mules. He smiled at one of them, Gabby Winslow, and he said, "I hear you got lucky at cards last night, Gabby."

"Skill, Ben, that's all it be. What brings you out here to smell mule crap?"

"I'm looking for Danny Bellcone."

"I'm right here, sheriff," said Bellcone from one of the back stalls.

Ambling back, Sheriff Taylor said quietly, "Heard about that shouting match you had with Tremane."

"Some law against that?"

"Look, Danny, I know you've got cause to hate Joshua Tremane. I also know you're a hard worker . . . want to make something of yourself."

"Just why are you here, sheriff?"

"About what happened over at that church."

"Yeah?" questioned Danny Bellcone, "I heard some windows got broken."

Either Danny, he mused, wasn't involved in what happened, or he was damned good at hiding his feelings. As his habit was, Ben Taylor brought up his right hand and tipped his brown Stetson back to reveal the thinning hairline, with his left hooked in the gunbelt by the leathered Colt's Lightning. He watched for a moment as Danny Bellcone worked on the harness draped over the back of the mule twitching its ears distastefully and looking back at what was happening. "Look, Danny, I went over to the Moonlight Tavern, had a talk with Steuben about what took place Sunday morning. Afterwards, after you were through jawing with Tremane, you and the others bellied up to the bar again and were bragging about how you were going to get even with Tremane."

"We were liquored up."

"Reckon so."

"Shucks, I might have said a lot of things . . . some of which I can't remember at this particular moment. But, sheriff, it wasn't me going over to that church and busting any windows."

"What about the others?"

"My brother, Mickey, cut out earlier to go fishing . . ."

"That leaves three other muleskinners. As I was told, Dickey, Cavanaugh, and Olsen."

"Sure, they were hot to go after Tremane; but they didn't. Yeah, me and Cavanaugh stayed there, at the Moonlight . . ."

"Yup, what Steuben told me. That Dickey and Olsen cut out."

"Look, Sheriff Taylor, I don't need anyone to fight my battles for me. Sure I was mad at that rancher. But I told him plain out in the street I wasn't gonna chase after . . . Melissa. Told him flat out, Sheriff. Sid Mason was there; he'll back me up."

"All I'm saying, son, is that was some expensive breakage over at that church—those windows. They were paid for and shipped in from St. Louis by order of Tremane. Hell, everyone in the valley knows that. We're talking about forty dollars damage here."

"For two windows?"

"I know, awful steep."

"Could be that Dickey and Olsen did break them," said Danny Bellcone. "Could be at that. As I said, I don't need anybody to fight my battles, leastwise a couple of drunken muleskinners. I'll see you get the money, Sheriff."

"Good enough, Danny," Ben Taylor said around a grin. "This is more or less a case of malicious mischief. But you know how the locals feel about muleskinners, that mostly they're riffraff and such."

"Maybe so, but Tremane thinks I'm worse than that."

"He still eats at you."

"Mostly it's like trying to fight the wind. Him with all that money and land . . . and able to buy what he wants. You'd think, sheriff, Tremane being sick like this, he'd let go of things."

"You'd think so. Drop by my office after you've squared this away, Danny. And, son, I'll sure tell everyone you had no part in what happened over at the church."

Back on main street, Ben Taylor saw by a clock in the display window of Miller's Gunshop it was around midmorning, and most generally at this time he'd take a coffee break at one of the cafes. His being cornered by the mayor and other indignant citizens earlier this morning kept the sheriff on the boardwalk and heading for his office. Along with this little incident involving Danny Bellcone, another part of his thoughts were on a recent holdup on the main road running up into the Tobacco Roots. The fact the holdup happened down in the valley meant highwaymen were getting a little bolder. Was it possible, he pondered, that Sheriff Plummer was turning a blind eye to these robberies? Turning into his office squatting next to Turner's Funeral Home, he glanced at deputy sheriff Mel Stern sorting through the mail.

"Heard about that big window breaking caper, Ben."

"That so," he said edgily. "I sure got told about it this morning. You'd think murder'd been done all because Joshua Tremane was there."

"Kind of funny that Tremane didn't stick around to press charges."

"Heard he picked up his daughter outside of town and skedaddled back to the Double Tree. Did Reese and Pickitt leave yet?" These were his other deputies, and Sheriff Taylor had given instructions that they were to ride out to the western fringes of the valley and pick a suitable spot to watch the road being used by freighting outfits, this just in the off chance they'd encounter a few highwaymen.

"Long before sunup, Ben." He swung toward the other desk and picked up his hat and some legal documents. "Should be back sometime this afternoon."

"You serving papers on Clyde Fremont?"

"You don't have to tell me to watch out for his dogs."

Ben Taylor's soft laughter followed Deputy Sheriff Mel Stern outside, and then it faded when he slumped down behind his desk. Removing the stub of cigar from his mouth, he crunched it out in an ashtray. A glance at the mail told him there was nothing of immediate importance. He leaned back in the swivel chair and propped a leg on the desk, letting a studious glimmer filter into his eyes.

Though it was still midsummer, he couldn't help noticing that fewer prospective miners were passing through on their way up to the gold camps. By this he supposed most of what gold there was had been found, and by men scratching amongst the creeks and shallow diggings. To go deeper would require large machinery, which meant that after a while the money men would be forcing their way in. But not here at Ennis. It wouldn't be long, he felt, before this town would settle back into its old ways, a thought which filled Ben Taylor with considerable unease.

There were others hereabouts besides Joshua Tremane who had broken the law on occasion. Sometimes Ben Taylor had simply looked the other way. Now with this long spate of prosperity a lot of past misdeeds had been swept under the rug. While the avalanche of travelers had caused the sheriff of Madison County to be confronted with new problems. Merchants who'd been struggling before, had made secret deals just to stay in business, and had gained respectability. Just the other day he'd listened to talk of expansion by some of them, even of building a courthouse and other evidence of civilization.

"Damned fools are blinded to everything but the present moment."

Grimacing, he opened a desk drawer and lifted out a cigar. He lit it and inhaled expansively, knowing that if hard times suddenly struck, it would be the last of his smoking dime cigars. As for the fine citizens of Ennis, those who'd done wrong before couldn't change the past. However, they could change the future. The trouble was, most of them thought the future was some far and distant point in time. Where actually, and this was Sheriff Ben D. Taylor's notion, the future was but a heartbeat away. What have we got, a few months at the most before things go to hell up in the Tobacco Roots, if that. Then what?

"As Joshua Tremane is always spouting to the parishioners over at the Episcopal Church . . . these folks have laid foundations of clay. But no way you can tell them otherwise."

Rising, he stepped to a window. Hate to see, he mused, the bottom drop out. Or maybe it's just me, that I see things differently. Maybe that's the trouble with being in the law business, that you only look for the dark side of a man's nature, or things. That just maybe going to church more often would lift my spirits.

"Nope, Ben Taylor, the signs are plain for everyone to see. Trouble is coming to the Madison Valley. And I'm wagering before leaf turning time."

Barely a year ago Danny Bellcone had gotten into the freighting business. At the time he'd been at the crossroads of his life, in one hand holding the money he'd gotten for the Bellcone homestead, blood money as he called it then, and with Danny having to look out for his younger brother, Mickey. For a while he had hung around Ennis to get the lay of things, couldn't help noticing that the big freighting outfits were looking for muleskinners. But instead of hiring on, Danny had headed over to Red Lodge where prices weren't so high. The four wagons and mules he'd purchased had pretty much wiped him out, with what he had to pay in wages for taking on three idlers from there, who by chance were still working for him, quiet Art Dickey, somewhat rotund Erik Olsen, and Link Cavanaugh, a drifting cowpuncher who wanted to see what Virginia City was all about. Upon returning to the Madison Valley, he'd struck up a deal with the Hoaglund Freighting Co. A summer later he had purchased still another wagon and turned the reins of it over to Mickey Bellcone.

And it was a summer ago that he came sauntering down an Ennis street one day to first set eyes upon Melissa Tremane. Actually it was Joshua Tremane's daughter making the first eye contact, even though at the time Danny Bellcone realized she was something special, with those big luminous eyes and willowy figure, and just a shade younger than he was. A couple of days later he ran into Melissa again, and before he knew it he'd hired a buggy and taken Melissa Tremane out for a Sunday drive along the river. From there it commenced into him looking for Melissa whenever he came back from the Tobacco Root diggings.

"Then all hell broke loose," he said bitterly, as Melissa soon left town and Danny found himself being cornered in a local saloon by a half dozen Double Tree waddies. Inwardly he would never forget that hammering, with the scar cutting around the upper part of his left eye, a reminder of it every time he looked in a mirror to shave.

With winter settling in late and easing off barely a month ago to free up the mountain passes, there'd been plenty of time for Danny Bellcone to ponder over how he felt about Melissa Tremane. He'd concluded that she was the pushy type, and though kind of pretty, liked to have her way. Just as her pa seemed to have things sewed up around the valley. What kind of got to him was Melissa keeping on writing him letters, sometimes just short notes to tell him of how she felt about their relationship. He hadn't replied to any of them as he had a tentative way of scrawling words on crinkled paper. Or it could be that Danny Bellcone realized their deep friendship was doomed by what her father had done to him. How do you get back at a man hobbling around on crutches? Kick them out from under Joshua Tremane so's he'd fall on his fat behind in a mud puddle. While back there this past Sunday morning it had been liquor more than anything that had made him say those bold words to the rancher. For by nature Danny Bellcone was soft-spoken, but a young man knowing he was going to make his mark in life.

Just thinking of Melissa again, and the encounter a few moments ago with the sheriff of Madison Valley, deepened his scowling mood when he came around the stable and found Dickey and Olsen tending to their mules. When they sighted Danny, Erik Olsen said in a thick Norse voice, "Uff da, I think the boss found out it was us going over to that church."

"Morning, Danny," Art Dickey said cheerfully, as he edged to the far side of the mule he as harnessing.

"A shouting match is one thing, damnit," said Danny, "but you had no call to break them windows."

"Would it help if I said the devil made us do it . . . devil booze, that is."

"Art, don't try to weasel out of this. Damnit, the whole blamed town is accusing me of doing it."

"Now, Danny," said Erik Olsen, "me and Art will set things right."

"Forty buckeroos will set things right."

"Forty . . . bucks?"

"Yup!"

"But they was just a pair of itty-bitty little windows."

"Shipped in by Tremane for that church," Danny informed the pair of them. Then he caught a glimpse of his brother trying to hide behind one of the wagons, and his anger flaring, Danny yelled, "Get your behind over here, Mickey."

"We told Mickey not to say anything."

"Fine ways you're teaching my brother."

Atop Mickey Bellcone's round head was perched a shapeless felt hat with a red feather in the hatband, and he had freckles showing through the deep summery tan. He was sort of plump and a few inches shorter than his brother, Danny, standing five-eleven. He was a yonker everyone cottoned to liking at first glance, but if Mickey had any failings it was his enjoyment of a practical joke, be it on him or others.

He replied in a stammering voice to his brother's accusing eyes, "I promised to button my lip about this, Danny. Didn't . . . didn't know it would cause such a ruckus . . ."

"Since you knew about it, brother of mine, the three of you are gonna pay for them windows. So fork up pronto."

"Aw, Danny," grumbled Mickey Bellcone, "that ain't fair."

"Just do it." He was handed an assortment of crumpled bills and hard coins by culprits, Dickey and Olsen, more reluctantly by his brother. "Now get them mules hitched to them wagons and loaded pronto. Soon's I get back from seeing the sheriff, we're pulling out for the Tobacco Roots. 'Cause I need to get shuck of this town and all its pettiness."

Danny Bellcone tucked the money into a pocket as he stalked away.

Just past the nooning hour the wagons belonging to Danny Bellcone and a string of others caravaned out of Ennis. It wasn't too much longer before Danny let any thoughts of the town dropping behind pass away as he set his eyes on the mountains shelving to the west. Once they were snaking upward through those mountainy passes there was always the possibility of running into highwaymen. His worry about this was more for his brother than himself, and there was in him this one notion that he should sell out and settle in elsewhere and in a safer line of work.

"Or at least get as far away from Melissa Tremane as I can."

She was the one who'd been pushing this relationship, not to say that he didn't exactly enjoy having her around.

"But that pa of her's . . . mean as all getout . . . and for sure he don't give a damn about us Bellcones . . . so get along, mules . . ."

Chapter Five

It was more to appease his neighbors that Adin Webb had joined the Bald Knobbers, a vigilante group trying to rid Taney County of lawbreakers. Taney County lay in southern Missouri, where could be found such hilly places as Kirbyville, Forsyth, and Branson, and the deep-gulched White River. Now the Civil War was just a vague memory to the former sharpshooter. After coming home, he'd boated across Hensley's Ferry, struck up the Springfield-Harrison Road to a ridgy place called the Snapp Balds, there to take up farming again.

Tiring of this after a while, Adin Webb had turned his farm over to a sharecropper and headed west. It was down in Texas and territories farther to the north where he began hiring on to do the killing of others. But after each killing he always headed back to Taney County, to use his newfound wealth to build up his small farm, then to while the time away in Kirbyville, with most every Sunday finding Adin Webb attending the Oak Grove Church. His attire while in church or when traveling was always the same, a houndstooth suit over a checkered vest, and the bowler hat.

Tonight Adin Webb was clad in different attire, this while astride one of his horses, a black. As had others, Webb had turned his coat inside out and the flour sack thrust over his head had eyeholes cut in it, but even so he hung back a little as the cavalcade of around a hundred men came in on the White River road. Inside their houses, folks living here in Forsyth heard the ominous thud of hooves, the creaking of saddle leather, and then the bald knobbers were spreading out in the public square to surround the jail, a crude log hut. They had come for the Taylor brothers, a couple of Taney County hardcases accused of murder and sundry crimes.

The first blow of a sledgehammer against the padlock on the outer door brought the moon out from behind scattered clouds. It also roused the Taylor brothers. Succeeding blows of the sledgehammer sent the moon scurrying for cloud cover and the cries for help of the prisoners tearing out of the barred windows all over the valley.

It had been taken for granted that Adin Webb would become part of this mob exacting justice against these murderers. But if his fellow bald knobbers would have left this up to Adin Webb, a couple of well-placed shots through those windows would have done the job in short order. He knew this show of strength was meant to intimidate those opposing the methods of the bald knobbers. When the outer door sprang open, the screams of the prisoners grew louder. Shortly thereafter the Taylor brothers were brought outside, lifted aboard horses and tied there, and now the horsemen poured out of the town square to thread northwesterly toward Walnut Shade while directed by torches carried by a few riders. They traveled nearly two miles before spilling up a ridge near Cedar Point—here they came upon a black oak known to all of them because of its enormous size. Projecting over the roadway was a thick limb some fifteen feet above the ground. With sinister purpose the cortege circled beneath the tree.

"The leader of the bald knobbers glared at Frank and Tubal Taylor, and then his voice cracked out, "Do you have anything to say?"

"This ain't right," pleaded Frank Taylor.

"Was it right you boys committing murder? I suggest you pray to God for forgiveness for your sins."

"No!" screamed Tubal Taylor as several bald knobbers grabbed him and began removing the ropes that bound his legs and arms, with a noose snaking around his neck.

Quickly the horses were lashed out from under the Taylor brothers to leave them twisting to and fro and against one another and their legs intertwining as they fought against the inevitable. Only when both of them were dead did the horsemen swing away and separate to head out for their scattered homesites.

But even before the dangling men had died, Adin Webb had spurred his black around and was heading out. He was known in these parts as pretty much of a loner. And he had never married. So when folks who knew him well hadn't seen Adin Webb for some time, they would only assume he was sticking close to his farm or had gone on some fishing trip, about the only thing he enjoyed doing.

Along the way he removed the flour sack and shoved it into a saddlebag. Shucking his coat, he put it on properly, over the woolen shirt and bib overalls. He had the same disarming set to his face as when he'd served for the Confederacy, though he was a little heavier. But he sat the horse well, as of a man used to the saddle. He found that being cleanshaven made a man seem of lesser importance, and even when attired in a suit, a stranger would take an incurious glance at the man from Taney County, before seeking more interesting things to gaze upon. He welcomed this anonymity. Especially in his killing line of work.

But Adin Webb hated to leave the seclusiveness of these Missouri hills scoured with endless timber and the places in between where a man could grow crops or simply set up a still. As he grew older, it was the money more than anything which brought him to distant places. Of a frugal nature, he'd salted away most of what he took in on these jobs, had ambitions of buying more land and maybe someday being called a country squire. Another ambition which Adin Webb had been muling over was that of acquiring a woman, but only when his traveling days were over.

"Maybe another year," he told himself, as the realization came that it was drawing onto morning.

He swung off the trail sometime later and let the black, water itself at a secluded stream while going farther downwater and picking a handful of blackberries. By this time Arlo Peavey would be milking the one cow, Peavey being a second cousin and a man he trusted. But it was the milk set to cooling in the well that Adin Webb thought about now, and how those blackberries would taste swimming around in a bowl of cold milk. Since his property lay about three miles farther to the southeast, he picked a hatful of the plump berries and set off again, holding the hat snugged against his protruding belly and thinking that it had been at least two months since that last letter had arrived.

That time he'd gone down into Texas, to the cowtown of Plymouth as he recalled, and to kill some free-lovers. He'd enjoyed this job more than others since Adin Webb felt wife swapping was a bigger sin than stealing or running a still. Another trait of Webb's was his ability to simply forget about the sobering fact he'd just killed someone. It was a wage-earning job, and he was simply a craftsman. There weren't too many of his kind around, he mused proudly.

When he rode around the gravelly road passing under a mossy-stoned bluff, there was his farmsite and smoke lifting from the chimney of the log house. He left the road to pass slowly through high grass thick with dew as one of his coon dogs came bounding through a split-rail fence and baying, and then the rest of the pack yowled his way. After being away for the better part of a week it felt good to be riding in, since he knew Peavey's wife always had the coffee pot on.

Then his cousin was there to take the reins as Adin Webb swung down and said, "Couldn't help noticing how good that corn looks."

"Been hoeing it some."

"Obliged you tending to my horse. Come up to the

house when you're done and I'll fill you in on what happened . . . back there at Forsyth."

"Mailman passed through yesterday, Adin—got yourself a letter."

There was a flickering of interest in Adin Webb's eyes when he made his way through the milling dogs and found the kitchen door, and Peavey's wife, Millie, washing dishes. "Morning," he said. "Picked us some berries." He passed on through into a large room which he used as his bedroom and a place to stow his weapons and belongings. By unspoken accord he made his own bed, though Peavey's wife washed his clothes and bedding, but she knew enough to stay clear of the one desk holding his papers and a few other personal things. He kept the .50 caliber killing rifle in a locked cabinet and other implements used to service the rifle. Once she'd glimpsed him cleaning the breakdown rifle, but never commented on it, nor would she or her husband.

The letter, as he expected, lay unopened on his rolltop desk. But first he removed his hat and coat and hung them up on a wall peg before easing into the cane chair. Right away the Bozeman postmark on the thick envelope told Adin Webb he'd be heading up to Montana. As he expected, there was a retainer fee in the amount of a thousand dollars, but the contents of the letter he opened and began reading gave him pause. It told the Missourian he could earn another ten thousand dollars by simply going up to Bozeman, there to await further instructions. "Register at the Klondike Hotel under the name of Jake Brown."

Always before the envelope had simply contained what he charged for killing someone, that person's name and where he could be found. Webb would come in quietly and do the job, to slip back here to Taney County. This was an arrangement that had never failed him before, had kept him alive, whereas the few others doing as he was, kept getting themselves killed. Could this be a trap? Supposing this money had been sent by a person or persons who were seeking revenge, for after all, he'd made three or four trips up to that Montana Territory. It was highly likely too that he was dealing with someone not trusting the sanctity of the mails, but Adin Webb brushed this opinion aside.

"Adin," called out Peavey's wife, "chow's ready."

"Be there in a minute," he said amiably. If the truth be known, he mused, this job could see me getting out of this line of work. Maybe this letter is from a high roller . . . that more could be made out of this than what's already been offered. For some unaccountable reason there came to mind his last job up there, his stagecoaching south from Bozeman into Madison Valley. It hadn't taken him long to worm out of the locals about rancher Joshua Tremane wanting to be the head rooster. He supposed by now Tremane had bought up the ranches of the two men he'd gunned down. There was also the big copper wars going on westward at Butte, gold and silver mining in other places. So a man with his unique qualities would be in high demand.

Placing the money in a desk drawer, Adin Webb went into the kitchen, lifted a stove lid and tossed the letter onto the chunks of burning wood. He found a place at the table. "Millie, you sure do set a good table."

"Got me a good wife," said Peavey. "I expect you'll be leaving again, Adin?"

"Expect so. This just might be the last of my wanderings."

"Sure could use you around here. There's this hunk of land we could buy . . . Robinson's fixin' on callin' it quits. Now you was gonna tell me about last night . . ."

"That was some sight—them Taylors dangling under that oak tree. But a man goes around breakin' the law, he's gotta pay."

"Amen to that, Brother Webb."

"Amen . . . and pass them berries."

Two days later Adin Webb and his cousin, Peavey, arrived at the railroad depot at Springfield. Webb untied the valise containing his breakdown rifle from his saddle, was handed a carpetbag by Peavey, who said gravely, "You take care now, cousin. An' jest make sure them lawbreakers don't backshoot you."

"Will be gone some time, as I'm strikin' up north a far piece. Like I told you, make sure that earnest money's in Robinson's hands the next couple of days."

"You still figurin' on buyin' all of his land?"

"Time I settled into being a country squire." A smile flared. "Figure right down here is that place of Jubilo I've always been looking for."

Chapter Six

Summer had passed into early August when the man from Taney County entrained at Bozeman. Instead of taking one of the hacks lined up out in front of the depot, Adin Webb hefted his luggage and set out briskly along the street. Having been here before, he knew it was a good mile and a half to the Klondike Hotel. But he needed to work the stiffness out of his legs, and he truly enjoyed this dry Montana wind which swept in off the mountains. The eyes of those he passed took in the houndstooth suit and checkered vest, rarely settled upon the roundish face under the bowler, figuring the sharpshooter to be just another snake oil salesman.

Painters on high scaffolds were slapping yellow paint onto the wide facade of the Klondike Hotel. Farther along Center Street Adin Webb laid amused eyes on a drunken miner hitching at his belt while trying to tip his hat to some passing women. The miner swiveled his head back the way he was walking only to slam into a hitching rack and sprawl over it. Two saddled broncs hitched there tried bucking away, and then Adin Webb was ducking through the obstructing scaffolds to enter the hotel lobby.

Once he registered under the name of Jake Brown, Webb knew word of his arrival would be carried to his new employer. This was a risk he'd decided to take. He bided his time, the luggage at his feet, as the day clerk tried to explain to one of the Irishmen clustered there that an extra dollar would have to be charged if a spare cot was brought into their room.

"But land's sakes, man, Clancy has agreed to share our bed."

"That bed, Mr. O'Shaugnessey, can barely hold two, much less three people."

"What do you say, Clancy, should we seek lodging elsewhere?"

"Why do we need lodgin' at all," retorted the third man, "The saloons never close and our train to Butte leaves at sunrise."

"Aye, lads, I agree," and with a smile, the one called O'Shaugnessey picked up his battered suitcase to follow the others out of the lobby.

Smiling after them, Adin Webb strode forward to say, "Leave it to the Irish to enjoy life to its fullest. I'll need a room."

"We have plenty of those . . . mostly because some of our guests don't like the smell of fresh paint. Jake . . . Brown?"

"From St. Louis. Perhaps you could do me a favor . . ."

"Yessir?"

"I'll be needing another room . . . for a lady friend of mine"—unpocketing some silver dollars, he placed two of them on the registry book—"say across the hall from mine."

"That could be arranged, Mr. Brown. For . . . how long?"

Some more silver dollars were placed on the lined pages of the book. "A few days . . . a week, perhaps. But this room for my lady friend must be our little secret."

"No problem there, Mr. Brown. Room 220'll be yours . . . and here's the key for one just across the hall, 221. And I do hope you enjoy your stay at the Klondike." The day clerk stroked his pencil mustache as he scooped up the silver dollars to have them find one of his coat pockets. Coming around the counter, he leaned to reach for the luggage, to be handed the one containing Adin Webb's spare clothing.

Up in the open doorway of his room, he tossed the day clerk another dollar. Then Adin Webb waited until the clerk was going down the staircase off to his left before he brought his luggage out into the carpeted hallway and closed and locked the door to Room 220. He went over and locked the door opposite, to carry his luggage inside. To his satisfaction he found the south window of Room 221 opened onto a balcony, and a short distance away a stairway ran down into an alleyway. This would be his escape route if anything went wrong. He had his doubts about the day clerk being involved in this, that most likely the hotel manager would announce the arrival in Bozeman of Jake Brown. On the way here, there'd been many self-doubts.

"Too much money to turn down," he murmured with some reluctance.

To pass the time Adin Webb removed his extra

shirts and other clothing from the carpetbag and hung them up to get the wrinkles out. The valise holding the weapon of his craft he brought into the attached washroom and wedged it into a small cabinet under the sink. Then he went into his room and found a deck of playing cards in the carpetbag and started playing solitaire to pass the time.

Adin Webb figured it would be a day or two before he was contacted by those responsible for his being here. But at the moment there was another matter to be dealt with, something that would require him hiring a buggy. For, if this deal panned out, it was time for him to close up shop on this sharpshooting business. Which meant having a little chat with his contact here at Bozeman.

It was Adin Webb's notion from the beginning that this killing was purely a business arrangement. Which is why the price for his services was so high, along with a gilt-edged guarantee to those who hired him that the job would be done properly. Knowing that he just couldn't go about handing out posters or placing advertisements in western newspapers, Webb took into his confidence a saloon owner in Waco, Texas, one farther north in Dodge City, and another here at Bozeman. These men let it be known to a few money men and some cattle barons that the services of a high-quality sharpshooter were available. It wasn't too much longer before the letters Adin Webb received from his saloon owner agents fetched him out of Taney County and do the killing of others.

But what he discovered over the seven-going-on-eight years he'd been doing this that traveling long distances and the habit he had of staying at the finest hostelries cost a-plenty. Lately, too, he'd gotten to figuring the odds, and had decided they were stacked against him. But unlike legitimate businessmen, he couldn't pass on his skills or sell his rifle to someone wanting to get into this line of work. Which to Adin Webb meant simply that he must bury the past, the implements he used in his killings, deal with the only three men privy to his name and knew that he came from Taney County, Missouri.

Catty-cornering just upstreet was the Gold Street Saloon, with harsh yellow light and rowdy music pouring out of its open windows and the batwings heaving shut. This was an overnighting place for carpetbaggers, spilling out to the small cowtowns during daylight hours, miners, cattlemen, and those employed by the railroad to keep the main line open westward to Butte and beyond. On his last and only trip through he'd hooked up for a couple of pleasurable nights with a pretty trollop named Sadie Blue, and he wondered if she'd still be around, again, probably not as the circuit kept these women hopping from town to town. Sadie Blue, it was a pleasure just saying her name again.

He brought his carriage past the Gold Street Saloon and wheeled it onto a side street, and at the next intersection U-d around and came back to tie up the gelding to a convenient tree, not rustling but standing silently under a clear sky. Inside the saloon, he was hoping, would be its owner, Casey Leonard, about forty when Adin Webb had struck his deal with the man, and now coming onto his fifties and probably a lot balder. Reminiscing now as to the character of the saloon owner—back then Casey Leonard had imported some high-kicking dancehall girls from Salt Lake, naturally to be followed at the same time by crooked gamblers and the like. After a couple of shootings the law cleaned out the place, but somehow the Gold Street Saloon survived this slur to its questionable reputation and kept its doors open. Or perhaps this was due to the fact Leonard had his hand in local politics, which was the reason he'd asked the saloon owner to be his northern agent. At the time he'd grown a beard, and when it was bushy enough, dyed it to a reddish tint, clad himself in cowboy rigging put on round-rimmed glasses, then to look up Casey Leonard. After he'd told the saloon owner he was the man who'd gunned down a certain Wyoming lawman, then hogging the front pages of most newspapers, no more questions had been asked.

Under the left shoulder of Adin Webb's hounds-tooth suit coat there was a holstered .32 revolver. He couldn't remember the last time it had been used other than for target practice. But it was part of his religion to clean the weapon every week. Once he'd tried wearing cowboy boots, but his feet were so wide the torture of even putting them on soon had him back to the more comfortable high leather brogans.

It was around ten, an hour considered to be the shank of the evening by heavy drinkers, and no respectable woman was out on the wending streets. But they were crowded with horses tethered out front of most of the saloons or in some cases along side walls facing onto empty lots. Webb's was one of the few buggies to be seen. He allowed a miner to precede him into the saloon, and upon entering, Adin Webb sauntered along the front wall toward the long bar as of a man thirsting for a drink. As he hooked a brogan on the railing, a cowboy so young of appearance the few bristles on his face more resembled goose down than whisker, said flippantly, "Howdy, pop, ain't you out a little late—?"

In a flat but friendly Missouri drawl there was this response from Adin Webb, "Just a nightcap, young fellow. It would pleasure me immensely to buy you and your friend another beer."

The cowhand laughed. "No offense meant."

"None taken."

"Sure, me and Arty could use another beer. You're a Reb."

"Been called worse."

"That suit, seersucker?"

"It pleasures this Missouri son to wear houndstooth."

The bantering went on for a spell as the pair of cowhands couldn't depart graciously before buying drinks around, Adin Webb's being brandy, not in a snifter but a chipped glass, which bespoke more than anything to Webb this was an unsavory place. With the departure of the cowboys, he had the front end of the bar to himself. But more customers kept arriving to come up to the bar or to circulate among the gaming tables. Shortly after arriving he'd spotted the saloon owner, Leonard, seated at one of the poker tables. And as he'd suspected, the bald spot was about the size of a pancake and throwing off a waxy glare. One of the bargirls smiled her way along the bar, figured Webb for a snake oil salesman, and wedged in between a man wearing blued suspenders and one clad in a black suit.

"Clyde, long time no see," she gushed.

"I ain't buying, Nadine."

Black suit retorted, "Neither am I."

"So, Nadine, get your big arse out of here."

"Be pleased to, carrot sprout." Other swear words carried her away.

Into his third drink, Adin Webb let the smile go away when the game the bar owner was in, began breaking up. Knowing that Casey Leonard often left to go home before closing time, Webb went outside and crossed over to keep watch on the saloon from a recessed doorway. Past observation of the bar owner's ways had also told him that Leonard would pass up the side street where Webb had tied up his buggy. With stoic patience he waited nearly an hour as his jaws worked over a piece of licorice rock candy. He always carried a supply in random pockets, and more than once, some left in an item of clothing had seen it come out stained after being washed. He started to move out of the doorway when a man resembling the saloon owner came through the batwings. He pulled back, to have Casey Leonard emerge a few minutes later to move along his habitual route.

Now Adin Webb went at a converging angle out into the street. He let the owner of the Gold Street Saloon move onto the side street before Webb picked up his pace, and aware now that he was being followed, Casey Leonard's stride faltered.

"So we meet again, Mr. Leonard. Easy, suh, I'm not carrying a gun."

He brought a hesitant hand away from a small handgun bulging out a coat pocket, let puzzled eyes splay over the stranger confronting him on this dark street, to say uneasily, "Do I know you?"

"We've met before, suh."

"I don't think so," he said firmly.

"Oh but we have, Mr. Leonard. Every once in a while I receive a letter from you."

"You . . . you're Webb?"

"Adin' Webb at your service, suh."

"Can't be? The Adin Webb I knew had a beard . . . a red beard . . . was a cowhand . . ."

"At the time, Mr. Leonard, I felt it necessary to disguise my appearance. Your letter fetched me up here."

"I . . . see? Is . . . I trust nothing has gone wrong?"

"Believe me, suh, there are no problems. As to my unexpected presence here, suh, I felt it necessary that we had a talk. My carriage awaits, suh."

Despite the Missourian's reassuring smile, there was this fear reeling through the saloon owner. Confronting him was the deadliest killer he had ever known. There had always been this feeling in him that someday Webb would come looking for him. He should never have agreed to help the Missourian, but he had, and right about now it struck Casey Leonard that he'd involved himself in murder plots. Sure, he'd profited from helping Webb. But tonight he would gladly be elsewhere than getting into this buggy with Adin Webb.

"Where are we going?"

"Mostly for a ride, Mr. Leonard. Want to tell you I've been real pleased with how you've handled things." He brought the buggy onto Gold Street and headed east. He kept up a running conversation with the saloon owner until they were past the few scattered buildings. He found a lane to wheel onto, then he brought the gelding up a rise and pulled under some pine trees. He tied up the reins. "Here, suh have a piece of licorice candy . . . got this craving for the darned things."

"No, ah, Mr. Webb, you . . . worry me."

"And why is that?"

"Quoting from Dickens . . . you're the ghost of Christmas Past . . ."

"Come here to haunt you. All I want, suh, is the answer to some questions that have been plaguing me. For starters, the last letter you sent me is somewhat different. Instead of it being just another regular job, Mr. Leonard, what it said fetched me here and over to register at the Klondike Hotel. I expect someone is to meet me there . . . and I believe you know who that'll be . . ."

"That'll be Tremane, owner of the Double Tree spread down in the Madison Valley."

"And what did you tell this Mr. Tremane?"

No clouds showed in the sky directly overhead and it was clear and balmy, with moonlight coming golden through the ruffling pines. Plainly he could see the expectant glimmer in the eyes of Adin Webb Though it was warm out, the saloon owner shivered inwardly. He was used to dealing with drunks and hardcases, could upon occasion double deal when the ante warranted it, had lived a hard life, and feared no man, that is, until tonight with the unexpected appearance of Webb. He shouldn't have given Webb's name to that rancher. But to turn down a couple of hundred dollars went against the grain.

"I'm waiting, suh."

"Look, Webb, you've dealt with Tremane before," he blurted out.

"Thought as much." His voice hardened. "Did you reveal my name to this rancher, suh?"

"Of course not, I . . ." Casey Leonard recoiled from Webb's handgun jolting against his stomach.

"You damned bluebellies are an untrustworthy lot. Our relationship is over, suh." The gun bucked in his hand.

The saloon owner gasped, stared through gaping eyes at the Missourian, barely felt the leaden slug from Adin Webb's gun piercing into his lower chest and didn't comprehend any longer, a hard shove from Webb that sent him spilling out of the buggy seat and onto the barren and needle-strewn ground under the pines. Then he died coughing up blood as his sightless eyes fixed upon a squirrel scampering away.

Adin Webb plopped another hunk of rock candy into his mouth as he stood there surveying the rear approaches to the Klondike Hotel. He'd left the horse tied out back of that livery stable, and on his way here, he had stopped for a jigger of brandy at one of the gaming casinos. He wasn't at all disturbed over his having to kill the saloon owner. Since it was his often quoted belief that anyone with a conscience hadn't ought to get into this line of work. Perhaps he'd survived these many years simply because growing up in that hard-scrabble Missouri country had rid him of such foolish notions as pity or the westerners' concept of fair play where two men faced one another before blazing away.

"They're dead and I'm alive is all that matters."

As for what recently demised Casey Leonard had told him, that his latest client was rancher Joshua Tremane. Could be, he pondered. Anyway, at this late hour the Klondike Hotel is awful quiet. He should have let that saloon owner babble on more, made him say that he'd passed his name on to that rancher. But at the moment that made little difference. He padded down the alleyway, thinking that once he did the rancher's killing work, it was only proper he turn his long gun upon the man. For he wasn't about to leave any unfinished business when he pulled out of here to head back to Taney County.

The staircase brought him up to the second floor balcony, which he eased onto, and stepped lightly until he came to a window he'd left ajar. Palming his handgun, he held by the window while sneaking a careful glance into the room. There was just enough moonlight for him to discover room 221 was empty. He eased the lower part of the window open and crouched inside. He closed and locked the window. Now Adin Webb shucked out of his brogans. Still holding his handgun, he crossed to the door and unlocked it. A cautious glance out into the hallway revealed that it was empty.

He eased into the hall, slipped across to feel along

the door and much to his relief to find the piece of paper he'd placed between the door and casing was still there, meaning to Webb that nobody had entered room 220.

Back in the other room, he pulled the shade before lighting the only lamp. "Perhaps," he said tiredly, "all this sneaking around is a waste of time. That Tremane just wants to be as cautious about this as this Missouri son."

It wasn't until the evening of the third day after Adin Webb's arrival at Bozeman that upon returning to his room at the Klondike Hotel, he found a note on the dresser. He read it by the light of a match.

"I'll meet you in the barroom . . . and don't worry, I'll be alone."

He touched flame to the sheet of paper and let it flutter into an ashtray. It had to be Joshua Tremane waiting for him down there. It would have taken the first day for a telegram to find its way into the Madison Valley and to Tremane's ranch, a couple of more days for him to get up here. During his solitary vigil here in Bozeman, Webb had come to the conclusion there was more involved here than just killing one man.

"But there's only one way to find out."

This time he stepped boldly into the hallway and passed down the staircase. The night clerk didn't notice Adin Webb easing across the lobby and over to the barroom door. It was exactly eleven o'clock, and he found only the bartender in the barroom. There were a few empty tables, and curtained booths passing along one wall. He checked behind him into the lobby, and it was when the Missourian looked ahead again he spotted the crutches leaning against a chair close to the last booth. He went back and eased out his handgun. He brought the barrel up and rested it against Joshua Tremane's neck.

"This isn't the way I like to do business."

"I trust you had a pleasant journey up from Taney County, Mr. Webb."

He stepped around to get a good look at the rancher and said, "So the saloon owner sold me out after all."

"Please, Mr. Webb, sit down."

"By rights, Mr. Tremane, I should kill you here and now . . . then make tracks out of here."

"Mr. Webb, you are looking at a dying man. Believe me, I would welcome your using that gun. But then you'd be out a great deal of money." Joshua Tremane gestured feebly to the opposite seat, forced a smile as the sharpshooter sat down. "I carry no gun, Mr. Webb."

"That's what I told that saloon owner. I lied then, as you're probably doing now." Grinning, be brought his right hand over and slid the gun into the shoulder holster. "It's a long way up here."

"So I'll get right to cases, Mr. Webb. May I?"

His gesture of consent brought Tremane slipping a hand to an inner coat pocket to withdraw a large manila envelope. He laid the envelope on the table, and allowed the Missourian to see the thick sheaf of greenbacks as Tremane removed a folded sheet of paper, which he passed to Webb.

"That, Mr. Webb, is why you're here."

Unfolding the paper, he glanced at what the rancher had written on it, then he stared hard at Tremane and said, "Quite a list of names. But I don't understand this other part . . . unknown victim . . ."

"Let us just say, Mr. Webb, that I have enemies. If these men were to be taken care of, killed you might say, naturally the finger of suspicion would point directly at me." He grimaced in pain, then reached a shaky hand toward the shot glass containing corn liquor. Only in the last few weeks had Tremane begun drinking a little whiskey to help him ease the terrible pain caused by his disease.

He went on, "The men I've named, you'll find other papers in this envelope telling a little about them. But it is important, Mr. Webb, that these men be taken care of in the order I've listed them on that sheet of paper: extremely important."

Frowning, Adin Webb said, "This will take some time. As you know, my method of operating requires patience and the right location, you might say. There's also the matter of the extra expense I incurred here."

"Yes, the extra room you rented . . . for your phantom mistress. I do applaud your precautions, Mr. Webb . . . and there'll be something extra to take care of this."

He stared at the list of names, said, "Now I know why you're willing to pay so much money. Killing one is hard enough. Or two or three. But gunning down seven men is something I hadn't counted on."

"Yes, it won't be easy," Joshua Tremane admitted. "But a man with your unique skills should be able to carry it off. You were down in the valley before, Mr. Webb, so that should help."

"I just hope nobody remembers I was there." He

gazed across the table into Tremane's watchful eyes. "Suh, there is too much risk involved . . ."

"A lot of men would kill someone for one or two hundred dollars."

"Yes, they would. And you're welcome to hire someone else."

"Mr. Webb, you know I can't do that. You're the best. As I stated before, my days are numbered. No . . . no, Mr. Webb, it is you I want to hire. Therefore I'll sweeten the pot; will another five thousand make you change your mind?"

"It sets me to thinkin' all right. Make it an even twenty thousand and we've got a deal."

"I could buy a sizable ranch with that kind of money. But, after due consideration I will give you that amount. Each time you use your gun the sum of three thousand will be deposited under your name in a Bozeman bank."

"Better deposit that money under the name you gave me . . . Jake Brown."

He slid the manila envelope across the table. "Here's expense money and a down payment of seven thousand, Mr. Webb. I suppose it will take a couple of weeks or more to get the job done properly."

"That it will, suh."

"Yes, after it's over I'll feel a lot better about things."

"You must hate these men somethin' fierce, Mr. Tremane."

"I'm doing this simply for the preservation of the Double Tree. I reserve my reasons for doing this for my own privacy. You must remember too, Mr. Webb, that if something goes wrong, you could involve me in this."

"If anything goes wrong, suh, figure on dying a little sooner."

Chapter Seven

Charlie Siringo would have bet his silver-plated Colt .45 that once he got out to Modoc in western Kansas two events would take place—either he'd have that killing sharpshooter in handcuffs or one of them would be stretched out on an undertaker's slab. Only it hadn't turned out that way. Upon getting to Modoc, his inquiries as to the whereabouts of former Union sharpshooter Cyril Lyndall had found Siringo being taken by the town marshal to a tarpaper shack just outside of town. That visit hadn't taken more'n five minutes, Siringo to be introduced to Lyndall, the Kansan gaping back out of white marbled eyes ravaged by cataracts, the marshal stating Lyndall hadn't seen the light of day going on five years now.

His return to Denver found Charlie Siringo barely ridding himself of some trail dust before Iron Mike Farley issued an order that brought Siringo farther north this time. He had never been to Red Lodge, an isolated cowtown just east of the Beartooths. But it was Siringo's kind of place, the locals being cordial to strangers, especially some of the younger women trying to figure if the Pinkerton operative had matrimonial qualities or was just another drifter. Of all these fillies, there was one catching Charlie's eye, a bosomy redhead who he found out owned a millinery store. But his hunt for that killing sharpshooter kept him looking for a roving cowpuncher named Boyd Snider, one of those on his list. He went out to the last place Snider was rumored to have worked, the LX Ranch, to be told of Snider having quit about two months ago. And since the ranch foreman didn't cotton to strangers asking pertinent questions, all Charlie Siringo could do was to ride back to Red Lodge.

"What you're telling me, Siringo, fits what happened a few years back in the Madison."

"Men being killed for no reason at all and from long range—"

"Yup, from long range," said Sheriff Eddy Pryor. "But there's always a reason. At that time two ranchers got gunned down. Never found out who did it."

"Where was Boyd Snider at the time?"

"Could have been most anyplace. Snider's a rover; had this sullen way about him."

"And from what I've found out as to his being in the army, can handle a rifle better'n most."

"I suppose you can hang that handle on Boyd all right. But I've never seen Boyd Snider pack anything bigger'n a 30.06. From what I've heard them bigbore .50 calibers cost a heap—and a heap more than Boyd Snider could ever afford. As for him going south, Texas for instance, no way, as Snider hates hot weather worse'n ticks and such."

"Who's head lawman in the Madison Valley?"

"Guess Ben Taylor still is."

"Anything else I should know?"

"Only that the Double Tree is sure hoggin' things over thataway."

"This a ranch?"

"Tremane's spread. I hear when Tremane passes gas . . . those owin' him dinero smile and say it smells like honey."

"There's a few Pinkertons I know do the same. And obliged, sheriff."

The sheriff over at Red Lodge had also told Charlie Siringo that it would be necessary to skirt the northern edges of the Beartooths and take Bozeman Pass, which would take him to Bozeman and there find the main freighting road heading south into the Madison Valley. Though Siringo came in to Bozeman on a passenger train, he hunted about for a good saddle horse.

Somehow Charlie Siringo had this gut feeling that he would find the answer to these killings down in the Madison Valley. But as always, he paid a courtesy call upon the local law, and here he found out about a saloon owner being killed under mysterious circumstances. Draping a copy of the *Bozeman Star* over his desk, Chief of Police Garver said, "Now here's another killing down at Ennis."

"Doctor Kreuger . . . murdered down along the Madison River."

Reading on, Charlie Siringo discovered the doctor was out for a Sunday ride with his wife when he was struck by a rifle bullet, it was later determined. The doctor's wife stated they were bringing their carriage along a stretch of open prairie just east of the river lying about a mile away. She further stated they had encountered noone, that at first when her husband had cried out it was her opinion he'd suffered a stroke, but then she saw blood staining the front of his white shirt, heard, as she described it later, the almost inaudible rumble of thunder. Though on this particular afternoon the sky was shy of clouds.

"Killed at long range, Charlie. Could be your man."

"Generally nobody goes around gunning for doctors. Lawyers I can see, but not those healing people. There's always a reason behind something of this nature. But we can rule out robbery."

"Why are you Pinkertons so fired up about this?"

"There were some killings in Texas . . . and other places. Figure I'm after a lone marksman. But in every case, Chief Garver, someone hired this man to do their killing. So they're equally at fault for what's happening."

The ride down from Bozeman was a pleasant interlude after all the trains and stagecoaches Charlie Siringo had endured the last month. The gelding had proved out to have an easy gait, and he would be reluctant to sell it once this business in the Madison was over. While his first glimpse of the valley and the cowtown of Ennis stretched out tidily along the river deepened the feeling he had about coming here, which he put into words, "Haven't seen the last of that sharpshooter in these parts. Hope it would be otherwise though."

The town wasn't all that large, but Charlie Siringo was just one of many using Ennis as a stopping place before tackling the Tobacco Roots and the gold up there. Right away he knew finding lodging would be somewhat of a problem. But troubling Siringo the most was of his being recognized. This had befallen him in the past, as he'd used various names and been known as a cowpuncher, gambler, cattle buyer, and on a few occasions an outlaw. As for Madison County Sheriff Ben D. Taylor, there'd been this lawmen's association gathering in Cheyenne some years past which Siringo had attended, and with Ben Taylor orating on the perils of being a county sheriff. Afterward they'd shared with other lawmen a bottle of corn whiskey.

Bringing his horse between false-fronted buildings, this on a wide, dusty street, more than once Siringo had to veer around freight wagons. Unlike most cowtowns, he soon began to notice there weren't too many friendly smiles on other horsemen jogging by or from those passing along the boardwalks. And the way of it in other towns close to the gold fields, he'd learned from past experience. The merchants would be gouging both local and stranger alike, and trouble had a way of walking in. Such as the killing of that doctor.

After Charlie Siringo announced his presence to the sheriff, his intentions were to seek out a livery stable. But upon swinging out of the saddle where other horses were tethered in front of the sheriff's office, the excited cry of a teamster whipping his wagon onto the street brought Siringo pivoting around. At a gallop the wagon came in from the north, the mules drawing it beginning to pull up in response to a hard tug on their reins. A crowd was following after the freight wagon, coming off the boardwalks and out of buildings. Then a deputy and Sheriff Ben Taylor came past Siringo still standing by his horse, and with the muleskinner yelling, "Jim Hardesty got plugged, sheriff!"

"Whereabouts?"

"Seven mile west of here—a bit past the Higbee place."

The deputy lowered the tailgate and clambered up into the wagon. He unrolled the old army blanket wrapped around the still form of the dead muleskinner. "Lordy, Ben, look at that hole in his chest. No question but that a big caliber rifle did the job."

"Earl, did you see anyone?"

"See anyone? Damnit no, sheriff, we was out in the open . . . and whoever did it would have to have more than cactus or sagebrush for cover. Our wagons were rolling along and strung out . . . and then . . . then poor Jim just fell off his wagon seat."

Sheriff Taylor speared the muleskinner with a wondering glance, "You heard a rifle didn't you?"

"Can't be sure . . . heard something right about that time . . . sounded like thunder . . . but distant."

He looked up at deputy sheriff Mel Stern, said, "Same as before. You think that slug's still in there?"

"Appears to be, Ben."

"If it is, Mel, it'll be a fifty caliber. You get our hosses, round up Reese and Pickitt and . . ."

"You thinkin' of formin' a posse?"

"I figure it'll be same as a-fore—the killer long

gone. Nope, just us lawmen to scout for tracks, empty shell casings, anything." Ben Taylor tugged worriedly at his weathered hat and looked about at the gathering, could see in the eyes of the onlookers the uneasy puzzling over this, and in some eyes flickering fear. They were thinking, he mused, maybe they would be the next one gunned down . . . a man suddenly going down out on the open prairie . . . the lawmen of Madison County unable to track down a lone killer. He told the muleskinner to bring his wagon around back of the undertaker's office, and the crowd to go about their business. As he started after the wagon, he noticed the other shadow stepping along with his.

"Name's Siringo, Sheriff Taylor. I was one of those at that association meeting held at Cheyenne."

"Yup," he said gravely, "That Pinkerton. What brings you up here?"

"These killings, I figure."

"That so?"

"The same thing's been happening down in Texas . . . points farther north. Someone gets gunned down, same as here. Nobody sights the killer. Next report we get, sheriff, it's happened elsewhere."

"If I read sign right, Siringo, you're saying the same man is responsible for what happened down in Texas. But there's a heap of miles between Texas and the Madison Valley. But you could be right as rain." They came around to the back of Turner's Funeral Home in time to help the muleskinner carry the body into a back room, the muleskinner telling undertaker Millard Turner any expenses would be paid by those he freighted with, and then he left.

"Millard," said the sheriff, "If that slug's still in there, I want it."

"Whatever it was, it sure chewed a hole in his chest. Okay, Ben, I'll get right to it."

Passing around the building and coming onto the boardwalk, the sheriff looked at his deputy riding up, and then he said to Siringo, "We could use an extra pair of eyes out there."

"I appreciate that," said Charlie Siringo. He went over and climbed into the saddle, reined around and loped alongside Sheriff Ben Taylor angling onto a westward-peeling street. They passed by a livery stable, where deputy sheriffs Reese and Pickitt joined them. Though the street ended near the outskirts of Ennis, the lawmen struck out across a field and soon found the main road.

The valley was more open than others, tawny and sun-burnished in places, broken by the main river with a few gullies and no trees to speak of, the wide beauty of the Madison spilling upward as of a bowl chipped at its top by mountain peaks. Back to the east there was a high bench below stubby foothills, opposite and the way they were riding it was more open.

Siringo's opinion as he rode was that it would take a man of stealth and cunning to carry off these killings. The truth of the matter was out along this road passing across the valley floor it would be all long-range shooting, if the muleskinner had been right about what had happened. They came over still another rise to canter past some lonely ranch buildings, the trees hemming it in swaying under a southeasterly wind.

"Wind from thataway could mean rain."

"Wagons ahead, Ben."

"Yup, still holding out here. Expect they'd wait for us to show. Or maybe for one more of them to get plugged."

The sheriff and Siringo, who'd been riding point, rode past under the watchful eyes of a muleskinner sprawled near a wagon wheel. Ben Taylor spat out some dust gritting his teeth and called out, "No sense you men squatting out here to get baked by this sun. I figure whoever did this is long gone. Gather around now. An' fill us in on just what happened." The sheriff didn't dismount but just sat slouched in his saddle to let everyone know the danger was over. This prompted some of the muleskinners to come in with sheepish grimaces, though none of them, Siringo noticed, put their rifles away.

"What the hell can happen, sheriff, when there's no cover around for . . . for at least a couple of miles. Just like that, wham, Hardesty let out a startled gurgle and went tumbling off his wagon; deader'n hell before he hit the ground."

"Never stirred afterward," affirmed another muleskinner.

"You must have heard or seen something?"

"Nary a sign of nobody, sheriff."

"But me, I heard this rippling sound . . . a banshee sort of wail."

"Damnit, Torgerson, it weren't that a-tall. Only a big bore gun can make a noise that raises the hackles . . . same's as when that sawbones got hisself killed, I hear."

"Which direction you boys figure?" As he asked

this, Sheriff Ben Taylor was squinting southerly and upon a distant hump no more'n the height of a man's Stetson while saddlebound. Now from the clustered muleskinners he received varying answers.

Charlie Siringo said quietly, "They don't know, sheriff. Such as was the case in other places this happened."

"Figure you're right, Siringo."

"Sheriff, what is the law going to do about these killings?"

Somewhat ruffled over the other killing, and the sobering fact he had found little to help him track down the killer, the sheriff said crisply, "No sense you boys loafing out here. So you might unlimber them bull whips and get them wagons rolling. For if this was outlaws, they sure as hell wouldn't allow that wagon to get out of here. He's gone, whoever done this."

Sheriff Taylor brought his deputies and Siringo away from the road, and here he issued orders that they split up and wagon wheel out for about a mile in an attempt to find out where the killer had lurked.

Siringo, with an easy smile, said, "I don't expect you'll find any too much. Especially if this is the same man I've been after. But where could he go but back to Ennis." He glanced at the afternoon sun hovering just above the western peaks, then southeasterly at low clouds moving into the valley. "As you said, sheriff, it might rain."

"Just our luck," he grousved. "Head out . . . and we'll keep at this until it's pitch dark out or a rain washes out anything we chance upon."

Chapter Eight

From a distance of about a quarter of a mile Danny Bellcone could recognize some of the people gathered in the cemetery. Strung out behind his empty wagon were his muleskinners trailing Danny into Ennis. The reins held loosely in his left hand, Danny's eyes lidded when he spotted Joshua Tremane slumped in a chair, with Melissa there and clothed in black. There was Sheriff Ben Taylor, and but for a few ranchers the mourners were a collection of businessmen.

During the past few days he'd been having second thoughts about what he had told Tremane, mostly that he had no intentions of interfering in the life of his daughter. Sometimes it was Danny's way to act rashly, to flare up, and upon simmering down afterward, to regret what he'd said or done. The truth was that he had no respect for a man who could order others to do his fighting, daughter or no. Last summer there was this hope born in Danny that his relationship with Melissa could become something more than a few walks around town or chancing to meet her at a local dance. Somehow his attitude toward her had been one of guarded optimism. Around her he'd guarded his feelings, been somewhat thick-tongued at times, and Melissa Tremane, she'd proved out to be one of those free thinkers, a woman who spoke her mind. Which was considerable, he'd found out.

"For certain," he muttered pensively, "she'd overshadow whoever she marries. Fat chance of this being Danny Bellcone."

He rolled on in to swing onto Beach Street. The others brought their wagons in around the clover-leafing pole corrals and into shadow cast by the stables. Knowing this was the end of another freighting journey, the mules didn't fight the traces as they were being unharnessed. By another building other wagons were being loaded, with Link Cavanaugh calling out to a passing hostler, "Who's being laid to rest out there?"

"That's right, you boys don't know about the killings." The hostler rattled on about Doctor Kreuger being bushwhacked on the flats south of Ennis. This had barely registered with everyone when he told of how one of their own kind had been gunned down under like and mysterious circumstances. "He got killed just west of the Higbee place."

"They find who did it?"

"Nope, nary a trace. And, too, it rained last night."

"So the killer used a rifle? If'n so, someone had to have spotted him."

"Not any ordinary rifle, Cavanaugh. A big gun . . . possibly a buffalo gun, you know, the Big 50 . . . something of that order. In any case, Jim Hardesty never had no chance."

"I know Hardesty. Easy-going, mostly a penny ante gambler."

"Don't make sense it being Hardesty. Coming in, you boys see anything unusual out there?"

"Down in the valley all we seen is pronghorn, jackrabbits, but mostly dust. What do you make of it, Danny?"

"Whatever happened doesn't concern us." He gazed over his shoulder at his brother, Mickey. "Make sure your mules get watered properly."

"Tend to your own stock," Mickey Tremane shot back sassily.

Art Dickey said in a pondering way, "You know, Danny, if I was you I'd watch my backside. That Tremane ain't one to let go easily."

"Come on, Art, Tremane's so pious it's sickening. I'll stay away from his daughter; an' he'd better stay clear of my shadow. As for Hardesty, could be he riled someone up. That doctor though, awful hard to figure. But let Ben Taylor handle all of this. I'll go up to the office and collect our pay."

Danny Bellcone strode away from the corrals under the watchful eyes of a man lingering in the lee of a building across the street. To those passing along the street, Adin Webb in that houndstooth suit and bowler was more of an amusing spectable than a menacing presence. After Bellcone went into the main office of the Hoaglund Freighting Co., there was this thought from the sharpshooter; how could one so young have incurred the wrath of Joshua Tremane? In the short space of time he'd been here Webb had found out in the saloons, a little about the young muleskinner, that Bellcone had been courting Tremane's daughter. Hardly something to kill a man over. But one thing he'd learned about the rich and powerful was this notion they were bigger than any government, be it territorial or this nonsense coming out of Washington City.

"A dying man will do most anything."

There were others on the list given him by the rancher. But crossed off were that doctor and the muleskinner; a random target. As for the moment, Danny Bellcone would have to wait, since the next name on his list was that of a man whose job kept him moving in and out of Ennis, this being Old Anse Pickard, one of the men riding shotgun for the Reese & Colmar Stageline.

"I always figure a man should be laid to rest just after sunup. Not late afternoon like this."

"It does make for a long day, this waiting around for a man to be laid to rest," agreed Sid Mason. Coming out of the cemetery hemmed in by an old picket fence, he paused to gaze upon Joshua Tremane's carriage heading back to the Double Tree. Handling the reins was ranch foreman Ozzie Browning, which in itself was puzzling to Mason. Ever since returning from Bozeman, Joshua would only come out of his rooms to eat or take his ease out on the front porch. Perhaps Joshua Tremane had simply given up, but that wasn't his style. As it wasn't like the rancher to let someone else drive that carriage. He's shutting me out, Mason felt.

He moved up to where Old Anse Pickard was waiting on the lane connecting up with one of the streets. It had been a long time since he'd had words with Pickard, longer than that since they were just a couple of waddies working at the Double Tree. Old Anse Pickard hadn't been all that old when Tremane hung that nickname on him because of that thatch of silvering hair, and this when Pickard was barely into his twenties. But he'd proved out to be one of the steadiest hands at the time Sid Mason had been ramrodding the Double Tree. Theirs was a friendship that went deeper than words. Old Anse had bailed him out of more than one tight spot in the daily and sometimes dangerous routine of making a go of a working ranch. And he was usually there to back up Pickard, who still had a craving for the nightlife, at the saloons and gambling dens they used to frequent. Damn, came this reflectful tug of remembrance, it's been nearly twenty years since we forked a saddle together.

They began ambling down the rutted lane, two men of about equal height, though Mason with a glance Pickard's way could see how riding shotgun for Reese & Colmar had creased his face into a dark leathery mask and maybe kept an alert sparkle in those china-blue eyes. Pickard wore leather wristbands and a brown shirt crosschecked from long use, and one of those wide belts decorated with silver conches but which were really just silvery-coated and flaking away to show the brass underneath. The hat was shaped to Old Anse's liking, tugged low in the front and wide of brim on the sides.

Sid Mason had on his best suit, a brown cattleman's single-breasted and a low-crowned hat, and a worried word for Pickard to his left, "Doc Kreuger . . . I remember it was him treatin' Lydia, er, Mrs. Tremane."

"Maybe that's the reason she passed away—what,

twelve years ago?"

"Thirteen."

"An unlucky number. What brought her to mind?"

"Stopping by her gravesite just a while ago."

"Me, I want my carcass planted out in the valley someplace," muttered Old Anse. "Kreuger gets gunned down . . . now this muleskinner. What the hell's going on around here, Sid?"

"I wish I knew," he sighed, and as they passed down a side street to emerge onto the main drag. "If you want to head over to the church for that free lunch, Anse, go to it."

"I've seen enough somber faces today. What about you?"

"It's been some time since we've gotten together. First, though, I want to get rid of this monkey suit. I expect you'll be barhopping . . ."

A smile worked its way through the seams of weathered flesh, and Old Anse said, "Expect so."

They parted, with Pickard going on along the boardwalk. As Sid Mason began crossing over toward the Concord Hotel, and the suite kept open for Joshua Tremane, he let himself go back a way to when Lydia Tremane had been told by Doctor Kreuger that she couldn't bear children. Kreuger, the Tremanes, and of course Old Anse Pickard, were the only people knowing of this. More than anything Joshua Tremane had wanted a son, and to be denied this had brought about his going to Salt Lake City. Around nine months passed, then he received a letter from the rancher telling him to bring the carriage up to Bozeman. When Sid Mason and Pickard got there, Pickard riding along as shotgun, it was to view Melissa

Anne Tremane for the first time. Later, in the barroom with his hired hands, Joshua Tremane revealed just what had happened at Salt Lake City.

"You boys must understand that what I'm about to say must never leave this room." The rancher looked away from his table, and then back at Mason and Pickard.

"Both of you know that Lydia can't have children. Just you two know this . . . and Doc Kreuger. But we went to Salt Lake for that express purpose. To get a child. But not just any child, nor did I want to adopt one. There is, however, a certain lady back there who consented to bear my child. And believe me, I had a helluva time talking my wife into this . . . arrangement. So, that baby upstairs is my flesh and blood. Heir to the Double Tree. I know . . . I know, Sid . . . and Anse, this would be deemed as damned improper to the folks back in the Madison. Which is why no one must find out about this. Lydia . . . once she got her hands on that baby . . . on Melissa Anne . . . she won't have it any other way."

"Joshua," said Sid Mason, "what you want is good enough for me."

"My sentiments," echoed Old Anse Pickard. "That Melissa's a cutie, awright. Well, boss cowman, why the long face? Ain't this a time for celebratin' the arrival of another Tremane to the Double Tree?"

That celebration, Sid Mason remembered with a smile, turned into three days of drinking and otherwise hell-raising by all three of them. This was the start of pleasant days out at the ranch. The trouble came later, when Melissa Tremane was around seven or eight. And all because the mistress of the Double ree, Lydia Tremane, couldn't live with the memory f what had happened at Salt Lake City. He'd heard ıat some people could will themselves an early eath. This was what happened to Lydia, a woman of onsiderable charm and beauty, but filled with the ainful memories of her inadequacies in that she ouldn't bear children for the man she loved. Her last ays were a painful memory to Sid Mason, as was her assing.

Getting now to the sudden demise of Doc Kreuger, his thought carried him upstairs to the suite in the Concord Hotel. First of all, it had shocked folks used o spates of gunfire and fisticuffs. For Kreuger had een more of a downhome sawbones than one used to utting on airs or overcharging for his services. The vay it happened was making everyone step lightly and ide more where there was cover.

He draped his suit coat on a wall hook, followed his with the vest, thinking of those two ranchers being killed the same as now. And like then and now, adn't the man he worked for made a special trip to Bozeman?

"Joshua, involved in this? Damned unlikely."

Although it had been Joshua Tremane buying up hose other ranches. But if Joshua hadn't, someone lse would have. While at the moment the only thing eeming to trouble Joshua Tremane was that muleskinner, Bellcone. Just a yonker, and hardly anyone to vaste anger or words on. Except, and this gave Sid Mason pause in his thoughts, the man he worked for vas dying. Could it be that Joshua wanted to get in a ew licks before they laid him out in a pine box? Others had, he knew, as this was the way of man.

"All this fretting over the past doesn't set well wit a man's belly. So he asked Ozzie to drive the carriag back to the ranch. Got to remember, Mason, this ill ness of Joshua's has caused him to be forgetful o late. Yup, probably be in the same mind frame if i was me laid up thisaway. Wal, Old Anse is a-waitir . . . and probably in some trouble about now."

Chapter Nine

The sharpshooter was seated with one leg crossed over another on a bench in front of Mitchell's Feed Store while jawing on a hunk of rock candy. He could have followed Old Anse Pickard into the saloon across the street, but knew that it wouldn't be too long before Pickard came out and barhopped to another saloon or dance hall. He was on the western side of the street, and it was just touching onto sundown. The garb he wore, a light brown woolen suit with string tie to match, he'd bought yesterday. It itched some in places it touched his neck above his shirt, but he figured his old houndstooth would last longer if leather patches were sewed onto the elbows.

With some amusement he watched one of the girls working in a large building set back from the street trying to talk a couple of miners into coming inside. Their loud braggodocio voices would set one price, she another, and Adin Webb figured this standoff would go on for some time. Despite business going on as usual in Ennis, he knew that his use of his Ballard & Lacy .50 caliber breechloader had set an underlying tone of fear. There had to be some reason for these killings, or motive, as lawmen and lawyers were fond of quoting. He especially liked what he'd overheard the sheriff say, this Ben Taylor, that neither of the victims knew one another, with both men not having any enemies.

"Look a little deeper, sheriff," he said in a silent undertone, " 'Cause everyone ruffles another man's feathers sooner or later." As for himself, he could have found out the reason why Joshua Tremane wanted so much blood to be shed. But long's the money was there, that's enough reason for Adin Webb. But after he'd tended to Old Anse, his plans were to lay low for a few days, along with hustling up to Bozeman to make absolutely certain the promised money was deposited in that bank.

That muleskinner had been gunned down at a distance of just under a half-mile. Which had been the easy part. Removing himself from the scene of the murder by skirting southeasterly along a dry creek bed had to be done carefully, and to where he'd left his pack horse. Since he would be in the valley for some time, Webb knew the importance of having a cover story, thus the botanical gear stowed on the spare horse and a few provisions in case he'd have to overnight someplace out there. Being a farmer, he knew more'n most about what book learners called flora of this region, had stowed in his packs some cacti and vegetation just in case he encountered anyone. There was no rifle boot on the horse he rode, nor would a lawman think to look for a breakdown gun. Despite these precautions, something could always go wrong.

Earlier he had watched the funeral procession wend out to the cemetery. Couldn't help noticing how much thinner the rancher had become since their Bozeman rendezvous. But Tremane's eyes, though they hadn't noticed the presence of the Missourian, still had that sullen glow. Maybe it's this hatred that's keeping Tremane alive. That being the case, he pondered, Tremane could live far beyond his allotted years. And he had taken particular interest in the man accompanying Pickard back to town, from the way he handled himself another cattleman.

He watched with idle interest as those miners were finally enticed by a girl of the line into that parlor house, and those availing themselves of what the saloon across the street sold in the line of liquor and beer, and then Pickard showed. Old Anse still had a sober gait to his walk as he sauntered downstreet, but as of a man taking his own sweet time since there was still a long night ahead. Webb held to the bench.

When Pickard entered the Moonlight Saloon, the thoughts of Adin Webb swung to the days ahead. From now on if they had any common sense those freighting supplies up to the gold fields would fetch along outriders. He'd anticipated this, as had Webb come to the conclusion that killing Old Anse Pickard wouldn't be all that hard. Since he knew what stage Pickard would be taking out of here in his role as shotgun.

Now Adin Webb rose when the man he'd seen earlier with Pickard came angling across the street, and when Sid Mason entered the Moonlight Saloon, Webb headed that way. He didn't know much about Old Anse's past life, but had heard that he'd been a cowpuncher in his earlier years. Odds are that Pickard had spent some time out at the Double Tree. Had to be this that tied the man to Joshua Tremane.

He entered the saloon to have a casual glance show Pickard and Sid Mason hunkered over a table up along the north wall. For a Wednesday night the place was crowded, but no more than usual. Three poker games were going, the only gaming action, and smoke hung curtainlike below the shading lamps. There were no bar girls as this was a place where if a man wanted a refill he headed for the bar, behind which three bartenders presided. A raucous murmur swept at Webb as he sidestepped a table on his way to wedge a place at the bar, and as he got there and was reaching for some coin, someone let out an angry bellow, this followed by a fist hamming down onto the top of a poker table.

"Thunderation . . . no man's that lucky . . ."

Across the table from the man who'd just spoken sat a sleek-haired man clad in a black hat and coat, and he replied, "Mr. Wicker, perhaps you've had too much to drink."

"Drink my arse," roared Wicker, a roughhewn and bearded man wearing a buckskin suit. "I may be a stupid buffer hunter . . . and not know how to read . . . but I know one end of a deck from another."

"Wicker," spoke up another player, this a cowhand, "Phillips has just had a lucky run. What I'm saying is, Wicker, he don't cheat."

"Them damned cards are marked," said the buffer hunter as a knife suddenly appeared in his left hand to stab out at the one called Phillips.

Only to have Old Anse Pickard, who'd anticipated just such a move and had been sitting nearby, clubbing his sixgun down at Wicker's hand to dislodge his grip from the bunting knife.

"Damn you!" Wicker cried out at Pickard, and he spun that way.

This time the barrel of Old Anse's handgun found the buffer hunter's temple, and Wicker fell heavily. When he tried lunging to his feet it was to have some of the card players grab his arms and another latch onto a hunk of greasy hair.

"Nobody pistol whips Butch Wicker and sees another sunup . . . nobody, damn you, Pickard!"

Calmly, and holstering his gun, Old Anse said, "Better cart this drunk off to jail a-fore another disaster befalls him."

They forced the buffer hunter through the batwings but not before he shouted back, "You're a dead man, Pickard!"

Up at the bar, a sudden smile peeled Adin Webb's lips upward. What had just happened, he realized, would give these folks something to focus on after he had killed Pickard. What would really tie it together was if Butch Wicker had in his possession a rifle of the same caliber as his. Further, this was no idle threat, since men of Wicker's breed never let a slight pass. He turned back to the business of drinking, which brought him looking at the man to his right, and Webb said pleasantly. "That was one mean buffer hunter."

"Those buffer hunters are short on common sense . . . and not much of a card player either."

"I gathered that, suh. Who was the gent stepping in?"

"Pickard – rides shotgun for Reese & Colmar. Been a long time since I've seen him and Sid Mason getting together."

This is providential, mused the Missourian, as he gestured for a refill. Here he is, Sid Mason, the last man he had to gun down. Obviously Mason works for the Double Tree, as did Pickard. The mystery deepens. It would help if he knew the past history of Joshua Tremane, though be could fill in most of it. For starters Tremane had no scruples about paying others to do his killing. Perhaps Mason, and again Old Anse Pickard, knew too much about the way the rancher operated. But where does the doctor he gunned down figure in? And another name on that list of Tremane's – Danny Bellcone? Adin Webb knew that he could stay up all night trying to figure this out, but one thing he knew for dead certain, and that was of Old Anse Pickard's riding shotgun on the noon stage out of Ennis and bound for Virginia City. Knowing that marksmanship needed steady hands and a keen eye, the man from Taney County polished off what corn whiskey there was in the shot glass and left the saloon to head for his room at the Concord Hotel.

On his way, Adin Webb studied the night sky filled with glittering stars. He was grateful that it had rained after he'd killed that muleskinner, so to wipe out his trail. Tomorrow he wouldn't need any rainfall, as this time his diversion would be that buffer hunter.

"Butch Wicker, you're about to become a wanted man. Which will make the rest of what I have to do a lot easier."

When Adin Webb climbed into his bed a short time later there was this unexpected remembrance of a refrain from a song first heard during the Civil War.

"– It mus' be now de kingdom comin'.
An de year ob Jubilo! – "

Eyes lidding into sleep, and filled with the eager expectancy of what tomorrow would bring, the unleashing of his Ballard & Lacy, one final joyous Jubilo brought him into an untroubled slumber.

Chapter Ten

In those riding clothes and with her hair pinned up under the crowned hat, Melissa Tremane could have been just another Double Tree waddy. The horse was one she'd raised, a grulla, and at first it had been skittish having not been ridden since early spring. Farther up on the slope where limber pines sheltered her from the early afternoon sun the elkhound was sniffing and pawing at some loose rocks. Spreading to the limits of her vision lay land claimed by her father.

What had brought Melissa up here was this morning's argument, her father denying her permission to go into Ennis. Her response had been that if she was to be a prisoner out here, she might as well have stayed back east. But Melissa Tremane couldn't deny that she loved the valley and all that it held.

"But my father . . . he's changed . . ."

Hearing her voice, the elkhound came wagging over before a tree caught its attention. While she kept looking northeasterly in the direction of Ennis and where she knew Danny Bellcone would be. Though she still loved her father, there were self-doubts about their relationship. At first she hadn't wanted to believe he'd ordered some of the hands to beat up on Danny Bellcone. It had all been so innocent, and probably the best summer of her life. Now she was twenty, older, a wiser woman, a woman unable to dislodge how she felt about Danny from her heart and thoughts.

"But . . . why? He's stuckup . . . stubborn as those mules he drives. Why? Especially after my father told me that Danny didn't want to see me anymore." Or it could be that her father had lied to her. "Dad's a . . . he isn't the same . . . even last year he was a lot different."

The elkhound bounding past and baying at a rider loping his horse through a distant draw brought Melissa spurring out from under the trees. She let the grulla pick its way down the slope, then she cantered toward the approaching rider, segundo Ozzie Browning.

Slowing his horse to a walk, Browning circled it around and said, "He was going over the books in his office. Then Ramos went in with some fresh coffee . . . found him slumped over his desk. Just passed out, Melissa."

"He needs a doctor."

"Won't see one. You know that."

"Like all Tremanes he's too damned stubborn." She jabbed a spur to bring the grulla into a canter.

It took them a good half hour to come onto the buildings, where Browning, a slope-shouldered and bulky man with stubble blackening his wide face, took charge of Melissa's horse as she hurried up the walkway. He brought the horses over to the corrals and turned them over to a waddy, and began that long walk toward the ranchhouse.

Her hat spinning onto an overstuffed chair, Melissa Tremane strode through the spacious living room with its high cathedral ceiling, and with her spurred boots chinking on the hardwood floor of a hallway. Emerging from her father's bedroom was Ramos, one of the Mex cooks, the worry of how he felt showing in his luminous brown eyes, and he said, "Senora Melissa, he wanted some morphine . . . but your father is still awake."

"Thank you, Ramos," she said worriedly. Melissa removed her leather gloves as she entered the bedroom and put them on the stand by the bed. She sank onto the chair, forced a smile for her father just opening his eyes.

"Ah, here you are," he said vaguely.

"Damnit, why must you punish yourself this way." She grasped his hand and eased the sheet up more. "I can do the books same as you, father of mine. Isn't that why I'm going to college?"

"Baby," he said, "oh, how I love you. How . . . how so many times I wanted to tell you this . . . and more."

"You shouldn't have gone to the funeral."

"Had to—Doc Kreuger was an old friend."

"There is another doctor in town."

"Bull, one . . . one"—he gulped down the pain—"is damned incompetent. Just passed out . . . in there."

Melissa Tremane kept holding onto her father's hand until he fell into a painful sleep. Gently she pulled her hand away and rose to meander into the living room. It was painfully evident to her that Joshua Tremane was no longer capable of running the Double Tree, but try to tell him that. And even more clear that he see a doctor. That would mean one coming out here. Glancing through a window, the shadows starting to peel away from the buildings told her it would be long after dark before anyone would reach Ennis, probably late tomorrow before the doctor could get out here. Even then, her father would put up a fuss, or explode violently as he sometimes did and send the doctor packing. The front door stirred and she turned that way and said to Ozzie Browning.

"Ozzie, he needs a doctor. Could you send one of the men."

"Turner's dependable . . . and don't mind riding at night." He hesitated, added, "This sure ain't your pa's idea."

"It's mine, Ozzie, and a damned good one." She held there until the ranch foreman left, then took from a back shelf of her mind the fact her father had been in his office, had been closeted there a lot lately. Just last week her father's banker had come out. She'd overheard them talking about someone named Brown . . . and Bozeman had been mentioned. Probably some cattle buyer up there. Or ranch business. What disturbed her now was the refusal of her father to let her help with the books. At his insistence she cut her teeth on them, and the tally books.

Melissa Tremane hurried back to her father's office. Some papers were strewn on the carpeted floor, and she bent to pick these up. Then she noticed the open safe door, and on the desk some ledgers. Knowing what the ledgers contained, she studied the handful of papers, saw nothing out of the ordinary.

"These have nothing to do with this mysterious Mr. Brown," she pondered, and took in the open safe door, which Joshua Tremane always kept locked, even denying his daughter entry to what the safe contained.

He's terribly sick, she knew, could pass away at any time. This thought saddened her, because her father had always been there when she needed him. Now the opposite was true. Drawing a chair over, Melissa sat down and opened the safe door wider. On a top shelf were two stacks of greenbacks, a few legal documents, below that on another shelf that old Colt's .44 her father always used to pack around, with her eyes landing on a small black book which had been tucked under the gun belt, and she reached for this. One thing she knew about her father was his attention to detail in that he recorded all of his business activities, even down to the buying of horseshoe nails. She'd found this amusing, and often told him so. Thumbing the book open, she found scrawled in Joshua Tremane's bold handwriting the name J. Brown, and sums of money to be paid to this man. Then she read in wondering order these names, ". . . Doctor Kreuger . . . Pickard . . . Danny Bellcone . . . and, and Sid Mason?"

She rose as the room was darkening and brought the black book with her over to a window. Kreuger; the doctor is dead. But his name's here? And Danny's? Danny's, and Sid Mason's, a man she loved no less than her father.

Though she'd been too young to remember how a couple of ranchers had been killed by a rifleman, she had heard all about how Doctor Kreuger had been gunned down. But the doctor's untimely death had nothing to do with her father. Hadn't Joshua said on their way to the funeral what a terrible loss this would be to the valley?

Reluctantly, but still puzzled by its presence, Melissa Tremane replaced the black book where she'd found it, and closed the safe door to spin the dial. Out of concern for her father she went to him and found that he'd fallen into a deep sleep. Every so often during the night hours she would look in on her father, as would Ramos. When morning finally arrived, it was to find Melissa camped on a sofa in the living room, but it wasn't until around eleven that Ramos announced a couple of riders had cleared the river and were heading in.

She knew little about Doctor Thomas Blaine, other than he had three children and had been in Ennis about five years. Sandy-haired with pleasant features and a quiet manner, he went alone into her father's room, but left the door ajar. Some time later he emerged, as did this pondering set to his face.

"Miss Tremane, I'm afraid your father has fallen into a coma."

"Is he going to die?".

"He isn't in the best of shape, I'm afraid. Just what medication has he been taking?"

"Some prescribed by Doc Kreuger."

"I'm not sure at this point, but your father could have acute ascending paralysis—more commonly known as Landry's paralysis, as he's having difficulty breathing. It starts in the legs and passes rapidly until it affects the muscles of the trunk and arms. So, Miss Tremane, there isn't much I can do at this point."

"You're saying the disease will eventually kill my father."

"I'm sorry. He could pull out of this coma . . . rally for a time. So about all you can do is make your father comfortable." He placed some medication on a table in the living room.

"You must be tired, Doctor Blaine. Ramos has prepared something for us to eat."

The departure of the doctor some time later gave Melissa Tremane a few moments to herself. She went out on the front porch and laid her eyes upon her father's favorite chair as the elkhound stirred from where it was taking its ease in shadow. There was every possibility her father would never regain consciousness. If so, he was the only person knowing the combination to the safe in his office.

"That list of names in that black book . . . what can it mean? Danny, yes, perhaps he would know?" Now her eyes softened when his name passed through her pursed lips. That she loved him she could not deny. And it could be, though this was doubtful, he was involved in some business dealings with her father.

As for Joshua Tremane, over a light repast the doctor had told her he could linger on for weeks, even months. There was also Ramos to watch her father when she left to ride into Ennis, there to find Danny Bellcone. In the past her father had hidden things from her, but in her was this growing sense of unease. For she hadn't been blinded to some of the things Joshua Tremane had done to become a cattle baron. Despite his puritan ways and support of that church in Ennis, the wrath of her father was terrible to behold. What he wanted, he took by guile or force.

"But . . . but had he hurt people . . . had them gunned down . . ." This admission fled from her trembling lips, was borne away by a gentle breeze rippling meadow grass. Were there dark and terrible things that her father had become involved in? One part of Melissa Tremane wanted to shed any thoughts of this, but the part ruling her heart and womanly emotions told her she must dispel any doubts from her mind concerning her father. To do so would mean seeking out Danny Bellcone, and maybe others having their names listed in Joshua Tremane's secret book.

Chapter Eleven

Adin Webb yesterday had taken the river road south for about fifteen miles, and then he began making a great circle to the northwest, going at an easy pace. He had plenty of time. Another reason for holding back was that out here a man in a hurry spelled trouble. Once he'd come under the scrutiny of a cowhand ridin' fence, had in fact stopped to jaw a little, and after giving the appreciative cowhand some licorice rock candy, he'd gone on his cantering way.

On his second day out he came upon a shelf of rock giving him clear view of the stagecoach road curling southwesterly before it cut back to lift toward the Tobacco Roots. The sky was a little hazy, and this worried the sharpshooter, the day warming so that heat waves shimmered near the horizon. He studied the gully and of how it would keep him hidden after he'd used the Ballard & Lacy. From his packs he untied a carpetbag holding his breakdown rifle, and some other implements of his killing trade. He left his horses nibbling at short grass and struggled up through loose gravel until he came to harder ground. Here a few large rocks were scattered about, the land before Adin Webb tapering off into prairie and the road no more'n a good half mile away.

"Shouldn't have any trouble sighting in on Mr. Pickard." The way he figured it, that stage would veer his way to give him a frontal shot. It would have been more to his liking to be farther away, but the haze ruled this out. At this distance his rifle going off would break some eardrums of those on the stage, and most likely pinpoint Webb's location.

"Lucky Old Anse Pickard had a run-in with that buffer hunter," the Missourian mused as he set his gear down.

Doffing his houndstooth coat, he set about piling up rocks to form a half-moon barrier about waist high. He worked slowly, still in about fifteen minutes sweat was staining his shirt. Then, opening the legs of the English hunting seat, he took his ease on it while noting the time on his turnip-shaped watch. The stage was due in exactly one hour and seven minutes. It was while waiting that most practitioners of his trade let what they were about to do get to them. Oftentimes they only winged or missed their intended prey. By the time they could reload their single-shot weapons any chance for a second shot was gone. Or when waiting their thoughts were more on getting away afterward.

Always at these times Adin Webb shut away everything but the practiced routine of setting up his gear and tending to his rifle. Now his eager hands brought the two sections of the rifle out of the carpetbag, the single metal workings and barrel and the wooden stock. He placed these together, firmed them with thumb screws. The German BOSS scope was zeroed in and already attached to the barrel. Assembled, what the sharpshooter held was a rifle weighing about thirty-five pounds. He laid the rifle down on his coat.

Next he extracted from the valise the tools needed to load the Ballard & Lacy, a powder horn containing Dupont powder, silk wadding patch, ramrod and a hardwood dowel. The leaden slugs used by Adin Webb were made back in Tany County, and were of a precise weight, this determined by weighing them on a gold scale. Just downslope a jay scolding at something from a stunted tree brought him glancing that way, but all he saw was the lifting valley floor, and up where the main road wended tortuously up the mountain-side some empty freight wagons so distant they could have been a column of red ants. He turned on the hunting seat to take note of his horses still grazing contentedly, knew he was as alone as a man could be.

Before loading the rifle, he jabbed the hand-carved shooting stick into the ground. He set the long blue-steeled barrel on the shooting stick, snuggled the hand-carved stock against his shoulder and let his right eye come in to sight through the scope. The road and surrounding terrain seemed to leap at him. He felt from this distance this was more a shot for a greenhorn than a man of his skills, knew without thinking on it that in a very short time the chest and most probably the heart of Old Anse would be ripped asunder. Hefting the rifle in his arms, Webb took a precautionary look through the scope at that approaching column of freight wagons still a far piece away, swung the barrel eastward to what he could see of the main road. Gauging by the heat he knew that traffic would be light, would pick up when the day cooled toward sundown. But that Reese & Colmar stagecoach had to keep to a schedule.

"Most any time now," he said, and laying down the rifle, he went to stand so that he was peeing downwind. The same hand which had just helped to button up his fly found a piece of rock candy in a coat pocket and plopped it into his mouth.

Reclaiming the hunting seat, Webb folded his arms and began the ritual of studying the wind—how it rustled trees, tugged at the grass and weeds between him and his target. As he'd learned while wearing Reb butternut, he watched the mirage, this haziness dancing and boiling above the earth and tilting with the wind. From this he could determine wind velocity by dividing the angle of the mirage by four. Determining this, he would multiply the velocity times eight, which represented the range or distance to his target in hundreds of yards, and dividing again by four, would know the clicks or half-minutes of angle he would need for windage.

The sun was tipping onto his left shoulder when

he saw dust boiling to the east, realized it wasn't a dust-devil but Old Anse Pickard bouncing around on the high front seat of a stagecoach rolling down a long grade, and now Adin Webb began loading the Ballard & Lacy.

Unhurriedly, and as though of their own volition, the farmer's hands hooked to the muscular forearms brought the ramrod tamping the large leaden slug deep into the gun barrel. The ritual of loading finished, there was still plenty of time for Webb to replace his tools in the valise as he spat out dust and sweet-tasting licorice juice. When he sat down on the hunting seat behind his rock cairn all that could be seen was the brown bowler and hunched shoulders. He was virtually invisible from the faraway road.

Patiently he watched the stagecoach being brought slowly up a steep grade, the coach on its leather undercarriage fading away behind screening hillocks, coming into view again, and closer. Then it came to that bend in the road, the span of six horses held to a walk and following the road of their own accord.

Adin Webb reached up and wiped the sweat from his forehead, with the overhead sun baking at his neck and its constant heat baking the ground powder dry and wilting the grass. He began factoring in the increasing heat, if the wind had picked up, knew the slight rise in temperature would elevate the mark of his bullet by causing the powder to burn more quickly when he fired.

"Easy," he murmured, "let them come in a little

closer."

Clear as if they were shaking hands he could make out Old Anse Pickard, the Winchester cradled in his lap, the one boot sort of stuck up to show the circular hole in the sole, the sun-burnt texture of the skin in the seamed face wreathed by a watchful grin. Now he made the decision to place his scope's reticle on Pickard's right breast, since it was his considered opinion the wind would carry the round right about six to eight inches.

"Another couple of seconds is all she rides."

Old Anse Pickard was mindful of a friendly warning from the sheriff of Madison County that he be extra watchful out here. After chewing this over on the first leg of their journey it was Pickard's opinion that he'd seen the last of buffer hunter Butch Wicker. The real danger would be after they got up into the Tobacco Roots where real bandidos hung out.

For passengers they had six would-be miners crammed into their stagecoach and one riding on top with all that baggage. Every so often Old Anse would twist around to glance back at their passenger wedged in between an oaken storage trunk and some valises and at the whiskey bottle the man was sucking on, and now he poked driver Bill Hertz.

"Hit one big chuckhole and that whiskey-swillin' critter'll go tumbling off."

Grinning through the black beard, the driver replied, "Just so's you latch onto that bottle when it flies by. You ain't said all that much so far, Anse."

"Give me any guff and I'll clam up for damned sure."

Bill Hertz laughed and tugged his hat a little lower. "You still worried about that buffer hunter linin' his sights on that fancy vest you're wearing?"

"No damnit, I just done my civic duty is all. There's these killings . . ."

"That muleskinner . . ."

"An' Doc Kreuger. Me and Sid Mason done some jawin' about that."

"That's right, Anse, you boys rode together a few years back."

"Yup, way back," responded Old Anse Pickard. He felt like a bulldog unwilling to let go of a bone, that being what Mason had brought up. He knew Joshua Tremane a lot better than most hereabouts. Figured greed and brass-balled gumption went hand in hand where the rancher was concerned. It was what Sid Mason hadn't said that troubled him, which wasn't like Sid, 'cause he was a man spoke direct and true. The unspoken part being that the man he worked for might be involved in these murders. Tremane's being close to death's door could have something to do with it. Opening still another door to the past, it came to Old Anse at that moment of how Tremane's wife had been a patient of Kreuger's. Now light poured in a memory window as he recalled Joshua Tremane taking his wife to Salt Lake City.

"Harking back?" he pondered inwardly, "Only me and Sid . . . and Doc Kreuger knew the true pedigree of Tremane's daughter."

That would hold water, he concluded, if Kreuger was the only one getting murdered, but there was still a puzzled glint in Old Anse Pickard's eyes when he brought his thoughts back to the business of riding shotgun.

"How's that miner doing up there?" Bill Hertz's eyes swung to Pickard, and then he froze when Pickard's fancy vest became all bloodied and he was thrown back against the coach, the Winchester spilling down among the harness traces, the heavy rumbling report of the sharpshooter's .50 caliber rifle crackling out of nowhere.

Driver Bill Hertz was aware of sawing back on the reins to try and halt his rearing horses, of Old Anse's dead flailing arms coming to drape bloodily over him. He didn't know as he finally halted the stagecoach that the passenger on top had thrown himself off the coach, and while the other passengers were firing their weapons at empty prairieland.

"Wicker . . . that damnfool Wicker killed Old Anse!"

He pulled the brake lever, managed to tie up the reins. Somehow he managed to stretch Pickard out on the seat as at any moment he expected to get hit, then one of the passengers yelled up, "Get us the hell out of here!"

"Over there!" shouted another, to have him and everyone else open up in that direction.

"He ain't after us!" barked the driver as he untied the reins and began lashing the horses around.

"Hey, we paid good money for you to get us up

to Virginia City?"

"We're cutting back to Ennis." And turning the horses around, he didn't wait for the passenger who'd jumped off the stagecoach to get back on as Bill Hertz brought his span of horses into a gallop. "Wicker will hang for this . . . damn him."

Chapter Twelve

By sundown, Sheriff Ben Taylor realized his only chance of capturing buffalo hunter Butch Wicker was to split those with him into three groups. They had left Ennis during the dying hours of the day, with too many men, Ben Taylor felt, and the slimmest of chances of finding Wicker when night really set in. Around him horses were beginning to mill and yank, for they seemed to sense the mood of their riders. There were still a lot of muttered oaths and lynch talk. He could see the anger flaring out of most eyes since many of them had known Old Anse Pickard as someone to depend on. Taylor had ordered everyone to dismount and check their saddle rigging, but a few were still astride their horses. But he didn't press the issue, since it was Taylor's hope that some of these men would call it quits before long and head back to town.

A nod from the sheriff brought one of his deputies over, and he said quietly to Mel Stern, "I count thirty-two riders."

"You want us to split up, Ben?"

"Into three bunches. I'm hoping Wicker is still in the valley."

"You know he's gonna head up into the Tobacco Roots and them gold camps."

"I know. Was me I'd do the same."

"And seeing it's Wicker, he'll have a cold camp."

"Moon's coming out full." He brought a hand up in the general direction of the stagecoach road. "Cull out ten men and head north off the road, Mel. You sweep westerly . . . but keep your men spread out."

"In a couple of hours we should reach those foothills, which is probably where Wicker's holed up . . . or once the moon comes out more he might strike up the mountain."

"He might." Ben Taylor finished tightening his saddle cinches, then unhooked the stirrup from the saddle horn and let it drop into place. A slight glance to his right landed his pondering eyes upon that Pinkerton, Charlie Siringo. First it had been Doc Kreuger getting killed, that muleskinner, and then Siringo had to arrive and go around asking a lot of unnecessary questions which only served to keep everyone stirred up. Imported killer—before as sheriff he'd gone along with Siringo's thinking. Since he knew of no man hereabouts packing a .50 caliber rifle. Butch Wicker, he knew as did everyone else, toted such a weapon. He could see Wicker pouring a slug into Old Anse as that had been the buffer hunter's brag. It still didn't set right in his mind Wicker taking out the others. But as Siringo had kept harping back in Ennis, it was just possible someone had paid Wicker to do this. But who; that was the double eagle question.

Placing a boot in the stirrup, Ben Taylor lifted himself into the saddle. He spurred up to rein his bronc around, and as he did so, a few broke off talking and others looked his way. Bluntly he stated his intentions to have them split up and sweep the valley floor toward the foothills.

"Damn, Ben, I ain't got owl eyes."

"With that moon risin' the way it is, Crowley, Wicker'll probably spot us a-fore we spot him."

"Fat as you are, Crowley, no way Wicker can miss." Others joined in the laughter of the man who'd spoken.

"Ricketts, you scrawny rooster, I don't have to take that," glowered Crowley as he struggled into his saddle cinched to the back of a large bay.

"When we head out," interrupted Ben Taylor, "everyone better keep their lips buttoned. Pickitt, you take charge of the other bunch—Reese, you ride with Pickitt . . . and that's it."

"I'll take the south fork, Ben?"

"Yup, Pickitt, mosey thataway past that gully, which you might sweep through, then out about three or four miles swing west. If we don't come across Wicker we should hook up around midnight."

Sheriff Taylor didn't say anything as Charlie Siringo brought his horse alongside. They were just south of the main road in a group of twelve riders strung out for about a mile, within eyesight, and most of them riding kind of nervously, since a lot of them had viewed Pickard's body when it had been lifted off the stagecoach seat. Meaning none of them wanted to have a .50 caliber hole bored through their chests.

"Go ahead, Siringo, spell it out."

"You're a lawman, Sheriff, been one a long time. So you know that in this business there's certain characteristics about a case you have vibrations about. What I'm saying is that Wicker's character doesn't fit these other killings. I gather it's been a long time since Wicker has been in these parts."

"Could be? Understand Wicker's got a cabin in the Madisons someplace, turned from chasing after buffalo to being a kind of a mountain man. But he did threaten to gun down Old Anse. And another thing, Mr. Siringo, you tell these men otherwise . . . that maybe Wicker didn't kill Pickard. Their minds concerning what happened are a closed bear trap."

"I can understand that."

"And if we don't bring back Butch Wicker, well, Mr. Siringo, I might as well keep on riding." The sheriff edged his horse away from Siringo's and fixed his probing eyes on the undulating roll of the prairie floor with its dark notches of gullies and draws, the darker stands of trees and rock formations buffed with moonlight. Once in a while he would lift his gaze in the hope of spotting a campfire on the lower slopes of the westward crags.

It was evident to Charlie Siringo he hadn't won the complete confidence of the Madison County sheriff. Couldn't blame Ben Taylor though, Siringo felt. Taylor knew more about the law than most sheriffs he'd encountered in his travels as a Pinkerton operative. The law in itself fit more comfortably in a courtroom than out here, where the man with the fastest gun or one gunning from ambush held the upper hand. Back at Ennis his inquiries about Butch Wicker revealed the man to be a blowhard, and possessed of an explosive temper. There was also this talk of Wicker having a Sharps buffalo gun. Though all of this added up to Wicker being the killer, Charlie Siringo knew otherwise.

"What'll happen if they actually find Wicker? Just hope the sheriff doesn't lose control. Otherwise they might leave an innocent man dangling from the nearest cottonwood."

Every so often as they searched for Butch Wicker, a dying star would cut a lighted trail over the mountains. In the deeper blackness below the horseman would scare up game animals, stop to reconsider what it was, and press on, but with a growing anxiety. Some of the riders still weren't sure of their mounts or they were getting saddlesore, the creak of saddle leather announcing their presence.

About two hours later or the time it took the moon to shimmer down from directly overhead, Charlie Siringo whistled softly, to have those closest rein up. "Wasn't sure about it before."

"About what?"

"See, in that notch low between those hills . . . in that treeline."

"A campfire," agreed Sheriff Taylor. "Can't be too far . . . maybe a couple of miles 'til we're there." He raised his drawling voice an octave. "Gather on in, men."

"What'cha got Ben?"

"Somebody camping yonder. Everybody gathered around? Now listen up. Me and Siringo will take the point—the rest trail in behind. Once we pass those foothills, we'll spread out just in case it's Wicker."

"And if it is?"

"As I said, me and Siringo will try ridin' on in. If there's gunplay, and Wicker makes a break for it, you men shouldn't have any trouble turning him back. Siringo, are there any objections?"

"I doubt if it's the man we're after," said Charlie Siringo. "For a man with Wicker's experience would think twice about building a warming fire just after killing someone. But, sheriff, I've no objections to riding in on chance of getting a hot cup of Arbuckles."

"That coffee, Siringo, might be laced with hot lead." A smile chased that worried look away from Ben Taylor's face.

Now they cantered toward the foothills. After a while and without looking, the sheriff said, "Been thinking about what you said . . . about someone paying Wicker to do this."

"I still say it isn't Wicker."

"Right now," Ben Taylor said gruffly, "Wicker's all I've got. You keep telling me about someone being brought in . . . a professional. My deputies and I have sure been keeping our eyes peeled for just such a hombre. But all I know is that Wicker had a good enough reason to do in Old Anse."

They cantered between that gap in the blunted foothills to come upon a heavily-wooded draw about a half-mile distance but under moonlight appearing to be closer. The upraised arm of Ben Taylor brought everyone except Charlie Siringo fanning ut to either side and holding back some as the heriff and Siringo spurred on. The draw seemed to e a lower part of the pine forest of the mountain, deep rocky gash knifing upward. The campfire hrew out pale flickering light, and figuring he had un out of riding room, the sheriff swung down as id Siringo. Tying up their horses, they walked in nder pine trees, catching a glimpse of a horse witching its tail and unsaddled, and the blocky orm of Butch Wicker squatting by the large campire.

"Shot himself a mule deer," whispered Ben Taylor.

"Smells good." Siringo slipped over and came in nder another tree, and about to fringe onto the low of the campfire, he unleathered his sixgun.

"Mind if we join you, Butch?"

"Taylor . . . Ben Taylor . . . that you?"

"Yup . . . and sidle away from that Sharps." The heriff stepped over a fallen tree and revealed himelf to Butch Wicker, the handgun held casually in is right hand.

Glowering over at Charlie Siringo, Wicker said ourly, "What the hell you sneakin' around here or?" He sank his teeth into the hunk of fried venion he was holding.

"Butch, I'm taking you in."

"Damnit, sheriff, I ain't done nothing. Or did hat damned Pickard bring charges against me for ussin' at him?"

"The charge, Butch, is coldblooded murder."

"What? What the hell you talkin' about?" He ropped the venison and half-rose, a bewildered ook in his eyes and jaw unhinging.

Stepping over, Siringo picked up the Sharps rifle "Been fired."

"How the hell you think I got that deer," snarle Wicker. "Damnit, Taylor, who got killed?"

"You ought to know it was Old Anse."

"Pickard? Last . . . last I seen of Pickard it wa after he laid steel alongside my head."

"Sorry, Butch," said Ben Taylor as he unhooke the handcuffs from his belt and came in closer.

"This is crazy, Ben. It don't make no sense."

"It does to me, Butch, and a lot of others. Bu we'll let a judge and jury decide all of this. Nov hold out your hands."

"No . . . damnit, Ben . . ." Then he kicked flam ing campfire wood at the sheriff and broke towar his horse. Only to be stopped virtually in his track when Charlie Siringo slammed the butt of the rifl at Wicker's head, to have Wicker go tumbling over Wicker tried to rise, managed to push over and fas ten glazed eyes up at Sheriff Ben Taylor, and ther his head slumped to one side.

"Would have killed an ordinary man," com mented Ben Taylor.

"Didn't realize I hit him that hard."

"He's a big man," commented the sheriff. Point ing his gun skyward, he fired off three shots. Ther with the help of Siringo he stretched Butch Wicke out closer to the fire and snapped the cuffs or Wicker's wrists.

Those who'd been riding with the sheriff came ir and put away their weapons upon seeing the mar they believed had killed Old Anse Pickard. After a time everyone began unsaddling their horses, anc after leaving their mounts in a rope corral, they brought their bedrolls under the pine trees. While Ben Taylor added more wood to the campfire to help guide in the others. Those with deputy Mel Stern rode in first to find Charlie Siringo cutting up the front quarter of venison the buffalo hunter had brought into camp.

Troubling Charlie Siringo was all of this angry talk directed at Butch Wicker, that if these men ever got it into their heads to have Wicker swinging from one of these trees, there was little he or the sheriff and his deputies could do. Some quarter of an hour later the rest of the posse was there. Now with the help of Sam Peldone, a man claiming to know the rudiments of preparing venison proper, Siringo used the frying pan he always carried and Wicker's to begin frying hunks of venison; and another coffee pot was soon hanging over the fire.

With a smile for Peldone, Charlie Siringo came out of his crouch and ambled over to where the sheriff was sitting with his back propped against his saddle and by himself. Easing down, Siringo said in a soft undertone, "I don't like all this talk."

"They're entitled to their say, Siringo. But it worries me." He dragged on his tailor-made. "You got something in mind?"

Glancing about at the men taking their ease in clustered bunches, Siringo looked back at the sheriff. "Most of them are worn out . . . and probably resentful of the fact we didn't make camp before. Once they've eaten, and shared some whiskey, it'll take the edge of their anger. But, believe me, Ben, it'll be a lot different come sunup. I've been places this has happened before."

"Expect you have, Siringo." But his tone was different this time, more respectful of what the Pinkerton operative was saying.

"This might work, that you hustle Wicker out of here before sunup. Maybe have one of your deputies stand cocktail guard . . . an' while doing so he can saddle your horses. From the looks of this bunch they're late sleepers."

"Might work. What about you?"

"Always been an early riser."

The sheriff and his deputies and Charlie Siringo, and the manacled Butch Wicker, were halfway across the valley before far to their backtrail Siringo smiled at a pallor of dust cutting this way along the stagecoach road.

"Here they come."

"Riding hard," said Deputy Reese. He swung hard eyes upon their prisoner. "We saved your bacon, Butch."

"Go to hell, Reese, and the rest of you. Cause I damn well didn't kill Pickard. I sure as hell wouldn't be addled enough to build a campfire."

Flicking thoughtful eyes over his shoulder at Wicker, Sheriff Taylor said to Siringo riding alongside, "The whole valley is in an uproar over these killings. They want blood no matter whose it is."

"The way of it, the pack. When it turns on a man it's a terrible sight to behold, guilty or no."

"Damnit, Siringo, we've got our killer. Folks hereabouts want to sleep nights, know when they're ahorseback nobody's gonna drill a hole into them. I know, Wicker don't seem all that smart; his past history testifies to that. But him toting that buffer gun is about all a jury will have to see to convict Wicker."

"We both know that, Ben. Set your thoughts back around seven years, to those two ranchers getting bushwhacked. Where was Butch Wicker then?"

"Come to think on it, Mr. Siringo, he hadn't arrived in these parts yet. But that was long ago and . . ."

"And who profited from all of what happened before? Records at the courthouse show Joshua Tremane buying their spreads."

"Had ready cash, I reckon—"

"Perhaps."

"Just what are you getting at, Siringo? And if you haven't heard, Tremane is awful sick of late."

"Heard about that. But someone had to hire the man doing these killings. So, you've got Wicker. All I can say is that I hope I catch up with the real killer before they pass sentence on an innocent man."

Chapter Thirteen

Sheriff Ben Taylor barely had time to circle Ennis to come in from the east and lodge Butch Wicker in a cell when the rest of the posse tore onto Main Street. They were strung out and arguing, a few swinging down and bolting into saloons, the main bunch letting it be known to people crowding the street they'd captured the notorious Butch Wicker. When they clattered over to the jail, the sheriff came out flanked by a deputy.

Ben Taylor had just released three cowhands and a gambler who received stern orders from Taylor to leave the valley. This town was a powder keg, that an attempt would probably be made to get at Wicker. Perhaps he should just let them hang Butch Wicker. It would spleen out their anger, but if that Pinkerton was right, they'd be hanging the wrong man. And come to think on it, ever since Siringo had ridden in he hadn't indulged in any afternoon pinochle sessions. With a sour grimace tugging at his mouth, Ben Taylor said, "Obliged you boys helped me capture Wicker."

"That was kind of rank, your pulling out before we was up, Ben."

"Well now, Thompson, you know I'm an early riser."

"Damnit, Ben, it ain't fittin' you protectin' that murderin' scum."

"What you elected me to do."

"There's times, Ben, when the law can look the other way."

"You want this badge, Miller, I'll hand it over. But if I do, you'll be guilty of murder . . . same's the rest of you. We've caught the man who killed Doc Kreuger, an' Old Anse . . . so from here on in it's up to a jury. Now quit milling them horses about before someone gets throwed an' go about your business. Me, I'm bone-tired and need a hot bath." He stood there, a stubble of beard on his face and age lines showing, a dull glint of worry piercing out of watchful eyes. In ones and twos they broke away, their anger blunted at least for the moment. They'd retire to the saloons and brag on how they helped capture Wicker. It was the drinking that would rekindle the flames of hatred. But as all men about to take the law into their hands, any attempt to break out Wicker would come after sundown.

He gazed at Mel Stern. "I'll wire Judge Benfield about this. Just hope he gets here soon."

"Never seen this town so riled up."

"Can't blame them none."

"Until Wicker is brought to trial we won't be getting too much shuteye."

"Then there's that Pinkerton."

"I take it you don't like Siringo . . ."

"Not that so much, Mel, but that he feels Wicker isn't our killer."

"You could," put in Stern as he jerked a thumb toward a Reese & Colmar stagecoach standing upstreet, "tell that Pinkerton to get on that stage."

"Could," admitted Ben Taylor. "But I reckon Siringo's a burr we'll have to put up with until a jury decides Wicker's future."

"Ben, that's a cut and dried issue; won't surprise me none, the city council authorizin' someone to build a hangin' scaffold."

They swung into motion, the deputy to reenter the jail and Sheriff Ben Taylor ambling down the boardwalk and toward a sidestreet which would carry him eastward to his clapboard house. While at that moment the stagecoach began rolling toward the sheriff, and with passenger Adin Webb setting twinkling eyes upon Ben Taylor for the briefest of moments. Then the man from Taney County sank back against the leather seat cushions and turned his thoughts northward to Bozeman.

With the arrest of Butch Wicker it was time to lie low, a week or two. Slowly during his stay at Ennis, Adin Webb had found out how the people really felt about the owner of the Double Tree, and of Joshua Tremane's character. The money, Webb felt with a quiet assurance, would be waiting in that Bozeman bank. As for the impending trial of Butch Wicker, he felt it would commence shortly, and this brought a quick smile that he shielded from the other passengers. For in Adin Webb was this sadistic streak coupled with an off-beat sense of humor. He could shackle his break-down Ballard & Lacey together while the buffalo hunter was still incarcerated in jail. Or wait until the trial was over and Butch Wicker had sky danced before taking out the next man on his killing list, muleskinner Danny Bellcone.

Sucking contentedly on licorice rock candy, the sharpshooter mouthed silently, "Just Bellcone and this Mason . . . Sid Mason. But I still can't figure the rancher wanting to kill one of his men. Unless Tremane's got some awful dark secrets."

Clearing a house belonging to Jason Miller, the owner of the local gunshop, Sheriff Ben Taylor laid pondering eyes upon the horse tied to the hitching post just outside the trimmed hedge sheltering the fringe of front lawn, and behind which lay his one-story clapboard. At Taylor's approach the horse swung away and whickered. But on its near flank he could make out Joshua Tremane's D-T brand. It wouldn't be the rancher, he pondered. Maybe Sid Mason or Double Tree segundo Browning. And probably here to tell him of some more rustling.

He passed through the opening in the hedge just as the screen door opened, to have Ben Taylor doff his hat and smile at Melissa Tremane. He moved up onto the porch as she said, "Sheriff, I hope I'm not intruding . . ."

"Not at all, Melissa?"

"I heard all that commotion as I rode into town. Heard you caught the killer."

"Appears that way."

"I . . . I . . ."

"Here now, pull up a chair. I expect Jessica treated you to coffee." He pulled another chair over and sat down facing Melissa Tremane. This was a different Melissa than he'd known in the past, a woman now, perhaps here to tell him her father's condition had worsened. "Should get out there to see Joshua . . . but lately things have been happening."

"I appreciate that, Ben. My father . . . has a list." She brought up a tentative hand and brushed a lock of hair away from her troubled eyes. "But . . . but it probably doesn't mean anything; perhaps it's just some business matters . . ."

"A list of what?"

"First the doctor was killed—then two others."

"Yes, a muleskinner and then Old Anse?"

Abruptly she rose to blurt out, "Ben, I . . . I'm sorry to bother you. Please, I . . . I must go . . ." Then Melissa Tremane bolted down the gravelly walkway, and with the litheness of youth climbed up into the saddle, to canter her bronc away.

Coming to his feet, Ben Taylor rubbed a wondering hand alongside his neck and muttered, "A list?" On the verge of turning to go inside and discard his trail-dusted clothing, the grimace deepened when Pinkerton operative Charlie Siringo came into view and strode down the walkway. "A bad time for a social visit, Siringo," he growled.

"That's Tremane's daughter?"

"Why ask when you already know that—" The sheriff reached for the latch on the screen door. "But if you must know, she mentioned something about a list of her pa's."

"Maybe a list of names?"

"Didn't stick around long enough to tell me that. Well?"

"I took the liberty of speaking to the mayor. Now don't get your feathers ruffled, Sheriff, but this was before Wicker had been brought in; on Tuesday as I recall. I simply asked if the town budget called for hiring some additional deputies."

"Under the present circumstances," agreed Ben Taylor, "I could use some. But without asking I know this was voted down."

"It was, Ben. If you authorize it, Sheriff, I could wire Denver and have some more Pinkertons sent out."

"That's mighty noble of you," Taylor said, "but I wonder?"

"Yup, I still say that buffalo hunter didn't kill Doctor Kreuger or that muleskinner. He might have gunned down Pickard. Just finished talking to Wicker, compliments of your deputy. Told me he was four sheets to the wind up at Tanner's Corner at about the time Doc Kreuger was killed—but couldn't account for his whereabouts as to the other killing, the muleskinner."

"At about the time," he said testily, "doesn't pin it down too much, Siringo."

"All I'm asking is that you or one of your deputies go up to Tanner's Corner and check out Wicker's story."

"Is that all, Siringo?"

"There'll be more," Charlie Siringo said softly. "More killings, I'm afraid. By the way, I examined Wicker's rifle . . ."

"So?"

"It doesn't have a scope . . . and Butch Wicker, I couldn't help noticing, is nearsighted."

"Damnit, Siringo, you're complicating things."

"See you later, Sheriff Taylor." Saying that, Charlie Siringo spun to walk away, with the eyes of Ben Taylor punching thoughtfully, worriedly, into the back of Siringo's leather coat.

One of the freight handlers employed by the Hoaglund Freighting Company came around a back wall of a warehouse and in search of Danny Bellcone using a flat stick to apply grease to a wheel axle. There were only patches of short grass in the large yard packed with large freight wagons, and a few grasshoppers hopping about over the hard-packed ground. It was in the low nineties, the hot wind yowling around the many buildings, though the corrals were empty as the mules had been taken out by the river to graze.

Danny Bellcone, sweat rivuleting down his

tanned face, and with his shirtsleeves rolled up above his elbows, shoved the stick into the can of grease and straightened up and swiped the back of his hand across his forehead. The others working for him, as was their right, were taking their ease over at the Moonlight Tavern. And his brother, Mickey, had saddled up an old crowbait horse and gone fishing upstream someplace for trout. Scowling at the freight handler striding his way through the wagons, Danny wished he'd gone with the others or fishing. Stabbing at his hat, he waved it at circling bottle flies, settled it again on his sweat-dampened hair when Watkins, he recalled, came up.

"I told Hoaglund we needed a few days off."

"Mr. Hoaglund ain't why I'm here, Bellcone." Between his yellowed teeth parted in a smirking grin he was chewing on a stem of grass, which he spit out and added, "Some hussy named Tremane wants to see you."

Danny Bellcone frowned as he picked up a rag torn from an old shirt and began cleaning axle grease from his hands. Melissa wanted to see him despite what he'd told her father, words that he'd often regretted. Ever since that encounter with Joshua Tremane he had shielded how he felt about Melissa from his friends and Mickey, his brother. There'd been days when he would hardly talk to anyone, with the urge growing stronger that he get out of the valley. Now, with the whisper of her name echoing in his mind, Danny realized he was in love with Melissa.

"But . . . it's over between us . . ."

"Damned if you don't look moonstruck," laughed Watkins. "And all over this hussy." The mirthful laughter turned to a grunt of pain and surprise when Danny's clenched fist slammed into the freight handler's rounded belly, to have him double over and gasp out, "Damn you, Bellcone, you gone loco?" But he'd blurted that out to Danny Bellcone striding away.

Coming around a warehouse, Danny set his face into the unruffled mask of youth when he gazed at Melissa Tremane standing by a buggy. If anything, he realized, she was more beautiful than when he'd last seen her, this almost a year ago, and not a girl anymore but a lissome woman. She wore riding clothes, the trousers tucked into Justins, a wide belt at her small waist, the blouse above that open at the neck to show a lot of creamy skin underneath, and with a flat-crowned hat shading her attentive eyes.

"Danny"—she held out a hand—"I'm glad you came."

Reluctantly he brought his up to grasp hers, instantly felt a shock of remembering static quicken his senses. Close like this, her presence seemed to overwhelm his thoughts, but there was still that honeysuckle woman scent and the deep well of Melissa's eyes telling him all he wanted to know. In a surprised corner of his mind, this thought came—she still loves me. But at the moment it was a painful remembrance, since it also served to remind Danny of what her father's men had done to him. As to why she was here, this thought was also flickering in his searching eyes.

"Danny, we have to talk."

"I expect," he began hesitantly, "your father told you what I said . . . about my not wanting to see you again?"

"In general terms, Danny. Danny . . . I've missed you so." Her grip tightened, briefly, then she swept a graceful arm toward the buggy. "I've brought along a picnic lunch . . . hoping we could go for a ride . . . to be alone . . . to talk things out."

"Melissa, your father hates me. Thinks I'm just trash. Us . . . us getting together . . . an impossible dream, Melissa . . . I'm sorry." He half-turned to walk away.

"Danny Bellcone," she said quickly, "I didn't go to all of this trouble of renting this buggy and . . . and bring along all this food. Please, Danny, my father's dying. And there is something else. But right here is hardly the place to talk."

"Guess you're right. But let me take the reins."

The place Danny found along the river screened them from the prying eyes of the town. Thick velvety grass carpeted the river bank and it was a place of quiet shadows and the scent of the river and the screening trees. While Melissa spread out a blanket and tended to the picnic basket, Danny tied up the horse but left enough length of rope for it to graze. He came down the bank a little and crouched down to sit with Melissa on the blanket, close but not touching, with each painfully aware of the other's presence and groping for something to say. The trees were alive with flitting birds singing out at times. Awkwardly he swung his eyes to her, and before he realized what had happened Melissa was in his arms with their lips coming hungrily together.

"How I've yearned for this—"

"It . . . it isn't right"—he pulled away—"it isn't meant to be."

"I never realized I love you so, Danny."

"I've got strong feelings about you too . . . but your father . . ."

"He can't control how I feel about you. That . . . we were meant for one another."

"All this will bring, Melissa, is more trouble. 'Cause your father's hatred for me goes deep to the bone."

"Danny, though it saddens me to say it, my father won't be around much longer. In his own way I know he loves me . . . and I guess I do him."

"Does he know you're here . . . seeing me?"

"He isn't aware of anything right now . . . his sickness . . . my father fell into a coma . . . perhaps not to come out of it. And, Danny, there is another reason I came here. I . . . just talked to Ben Taylor . . . the sheriff."

"I don't understand?"

"I was going through my father's papers. Found in his safe a book; had some names written in it. Yours was one, Danny. And Doc Kreuger's, and . . . and Old Anse. Pickard used to work out at the Double Tree."

"What did the sheriff say about this?"

"Out of concern for my father, I guess, I didn't say too much . . . left right away. Danny, did you have any business dealings with my father?"

"Nope. Maybe this is your father's list of those he hates. Two of those men are dead?"

"There was another name—Sid Mason's."

"Does Mason still work for your father?"

"Sid's a fixture out at the ranch." She reached for Danny's hand. "Maybe I'm being overly protective about this as far as my father is concerned. But . . . is it possible . . ."

"That he could be involved in these murders?"

"I'd hate to think that, Danny. He's changed, become wrapped in bitterness."

"Perhaps you should explain all of this to Ben Taylor."

"I tried. But give me some time to sort out my thoughts. You're a kind man, Danny Bellcone. Handsomer than you think."

"Do I smell chicken?"

"Oh, goodness, I forgot about the food. Now, would it be asking too much to ask for another kiss?"

He placed a hesitant hand on her cheek and then reached up and removed Melissa's hat, and then his own. "You know, you can have your choice of men. And I suppose you'll inherit the Double Tree. What I'm saying is that I can't match what you have . . . not at all. I'm just a muleskinner, but maybe that'll come to an end soon. I guess what I'm trying to say is that we're

worlds apart."
"I don't feel that way about us."
"You're sure making it tough on me."
"Perhaps a kiss will help?"
"Yup, it could at that."

Chapter Fourteen

Charlie Siringo reread the letter mailed to him by the Bozeman chief of police. It told of how the widow of a recently deceased saloon owner up there had come across papers which connected her late husband to a man living down in Taney County, Missouri.

"Adin Webb."

The hot, southeast wind carried away Siringo's soft-spoken words. Behind him some thirty miles lay Ennis, and by now Charlie Siringo reckoned he was riding over Double Tree land. He'd received the letter in this morning's mail, hadn't bothered to bring it to the attention of Sheriff Ben Taylor. Since he figured doing so wouldn't change Taylor's mind as to the buffalo hunter, Wicker, being the long-gun killer.

The key to all of this was the rancher's daughter, Melissa Tremane. Somehow this list she'd told the sheriff about contained the names of those her father wanted done in. As to how she'd come across it, Siringo had called upon Ennis's only doctor, and after threatening the man with arrest, was told that Joshua Tremane wasn't expected to last too much longer.

"Tremane lapsing into a coma could mean that his daughter has taken over. As to this Adin Webb, had no question but that Tremane brought him in, this sharpshooter. Back seven years ago, too, to kill those ranchers. But try telling this to the sheriff . . ."

Siringo felt these recent killings fit no pattern, served no purpose. Why did the rancher want these men killed? A doctor, muleskinner, a man employed as shotgun for the Reese & Colmar stageline—men having nothing in common.

Getting to Adin Webb, Siringo had checked out the hotels and other lodging places back in Ennis, came up firing blanks. Which meant to Siringo that the sharpshooter was using an assumed name. Back in Ennis and out here on the trail he could still sense the presence of Webb, the feeling coming to him strong the man was about to kill again.

"As I told the sheriff, more blood's gonna be spilled. All on account of a man gone mad or one with some secret motive?"

Catching sight of the main buildings, Siringo brought his horse loping in.

With a final worried glance at her father lying motionless under the coverlet on his large brass bed, Melissa Tremane left the bedroom. She sought her own room, but after a while decided she had to get out of this house and go for a ride.

And changing clothes, Melissa left to head out to the tack house. One of the older hands was there, the gray-streaked hair of Len Moreland lying thick along the sides of his head under his hat. Moreland's left arm had been crippled up when he'd been bucked off some years back, but afterward he'd proved out to be a good saddlemaker and mender of leather gear. Hefting one of the saddles he'd made for Melissa, he walked with her out to the corrals.

"Girlie," he said in a joshing way, "you look kind of peaked."

"It's not just my father, Len."

"Joshua any better?"

"He still doesn't respond. If anything, his condition has gotten worse."

"Doesn't seem fair, your father building this place up . . . and then to get sick like this. There something else you want to hash over?"

At a corral she turned to Len Moreland as he set the saddle down and eyed the horses milling about in the poled enclosure. The riata he held in his other hand he began uncoiling as she said, "You've been here a long time. Before I was born. My mother, she passed away later. But didn't Doctor Kreuger tend to her?"

"I reckon," he said guardedly. "Why'd you ask?"

"Well, afterward, I don't recall my father having anything to do with Doctor Kreuger."

"For that matter Joshua didn't have much use for pill-pushers. But Kreuger's dead . . . an' a hard way to go." The crow's-feet around his squinting eyes deepened. "Any particular reason you brought this up?"

"I'm hoping there isn't."

With a wondering grimace for Melissa, Len Moreland slipped into the corral. As the horses began fanning out and circling, he flicked the riata out and around the neck of a gelding. It didn't take him any length of time to cinch the saddle into place, and to watch the daughter of the man he worked for lope away.

"Something's sure ailing her?" he knew. And as Len Moreland coiled up the riata on his way back to the tack house, Sid Mason and three other riders topped a rise and cut past a cluster of haystacks. That she had mentioned Doc Kreuger held Moreland outside the open doorway, his thoughts leaping backward to the days after Joshua Tremane had brought his new daughter back from Salt Lake City. Later it was Sid Mason revealing to him the facts of Melissa's birth, and like Mason, something that was never talked about.

Veering his horse over, Sid Mason swung a tired leg over his saddle horn and dismounted. "What's ailing you, Len?"

"Her."

Mason gazed after Melissa Tremane passing into a distant draw.

"She got to talking about Doc Kreuger. About when she was born . . . and if her pa got along with Kreuger. Been thinking, Sid, now that Joshua's ailing she's got the run of the house. Could be she found some old papers."

"Meaning that she might have stumbled upon the truth of what happened. Could be, Len, as the bossman is more or less a packrat about details. That all she talked about?"

"That's enough, I reckon."

"We've got company." Sid Mason swung his horse around, and with Moreland alongside, moved toward a corral as Charlie Siringo headed toward them. "You looking for work?"

"Nope," replied Siringo. "Nice layout you've got here."

"Took a long time to build up."

Dismounting, Charlie Siringo said, "I rode out here hoping to have a talk with Mr. Tremane's daughter."

"I don't know," Mason said hesitantly. He looked the Pinkerton operative over, saw more than a seedy cowhand looking for work, couldn't help noticing the silver-plated Colt .45.

"Just the other day Miss Tremane came into Ennis to see Sheriff Taylor."

"Perhaps, but I don't think that's any concern of yours, Mr . . ."

"Charlie Siringo—work for the Pinkertons."

"Here," Len Moreland said, "I'll tend to your horse," and he took the reins from Sid Mason and walked the horse closer to the corral, but within hearing range of what was being said.

Siringo went on, "And you are?"

"Mason; Sid to my friends."

"Pleased to make your acquaintance."

"Mister Siringo, this isn't a good time to be calling on the Tremanes. Maybe you could come back another day."

Charlie Siringo knew from the hostile glint in

Mason's eyes that he would have to pick his words carefully. That he just couldn't come right out and accuse the owner of the Double Tree, since all he had to work on was a gut feeling as to Tremane being involved with these murders. A look of concern on his face, he said, "I know that Mr. Tremane isn't in the best of health. And I wouldn't be out here unless I thought it was important."

"Just what is it you want to find out from Melissa Tremane?"

"I'll handle it," Melissa Tremane called out as she swung her horse at a canter around the corrals. Reining up, she stared down at Siringo. "I saw you in town—as I left Ben Taylor's house."

"This gent's a Pinkerton," cut in Sid Mason.

"It's all right, Sid." She swung down, to have Mason take charge of her horse.

Removing his hat, Charlie Siringo told her his name, but before he had a chance to state his reasons for being out here, Melissa said, "I suppose the sheriff told you about the list."

"A little about it?"

Her eyes went hard. "And you're out here, Mr. Siringo, because you suspect my father could be involved in . . . in what's been happening."

"Ma'am, right about now I suspect most everybody in the valley. You've got to admit, Miss Tremane, that was no social call you made upon Ben Taylor."

"Easy, Siringo," said Mason.

"No, Sid, there is something I must tell both of you. There is a list of names . . . really a black book that I found in my father's safe. Your name is on it, Sid. And Doctor Kreuger's . . . Pickard's too. And . . . and Danny Bellcone's. It also lists that monies have been paid to someone named Brown."

"So . . . your father wrote down most everything he did . . . names of people he dealt with in business. Could mean most anything?"

"Or it could mean," said Charlie Siringo tautly, "that you and Danny Bellcone are earmarked for death."

Sid Mason paled into anger, and he started toward Siringo, only to have Melissa Tremane place a restraining hand on his muscular forearm. Her eyes went to Siringo.

"Seems to me they caught the man who killed Doctor Kreuger and those others . . . this Wicker."

"Butch Wicker, in jail?" Confusion danced in Mason's eyes. "All Wicker is, is a damned blowhard. Comes to town to get drunk. But a killer?"

"A few days ago he had a run-in with Old Anse Pickard—then Pickard winds up dead. Right now Wicker is in jail in Ennis; awaiting trial."

"And the only reason you came out here, Mr. Siringo," said Melissa Tremane, "is that you've come to the mistaken conclusion my father hired this . . . this Wicker?"

"He didn't hire Wicker. For the real killer is still floating around this valley. Ready to kill again, I'm afraid."

"But . . . surely not . . . not Danny . . . or, or Sid?"

During this exchange of words Sid Mason still had on his mind the chat of a few minutes ago with Len Moreland, in which Moreland had told about Melissa asking certain questions, the answers to which had been buried in the past. And something else, something that Joshua Tremane had said to him some time back, that he would do anything to protect his daughter's good name. Could that possibly mean murder? And if so, shouldn't Len Moreland's name be on that list? No, he debated, because at the time he and Len Moreland had been sharing that line shack, so it could be that Joshua figured it was only him, and Doc Kreuger, and of course, Old Anse, knowing about what had happened at Salt Lake. Now the doctor and Pickard were dead and buried and one other. But where did Danny Bellcone fit into this? Unless, and the truth of what the Pinkerton had stated stabbed home at Sid Mason, the man he worked for believed his daughter cared too much for Bellcone. It was this damnable sickness of Joshua's, Mason finally concluded. Still, there were still these lingering doubts, and he said, "What about this list, Melissa?"

"After I found it I put it back in the safe. Only my father knows the combination."

"We went up to Bozeman, me and your pa. On some secret business of Joshua's. Should have braced him then. But I couldn't. As we've been more'n friends for a lot of years. Just who is doing these killings, Siringo?"

"A sharpshooter out of Missouri—Adin Webb. Been doing killing jobs in other places. While you were up at Bozeman, Mason, did Tremane call upon a saloon owner?"

"Come to think on it he did?"

"Seems this Adin Webb is burning his bridges as that saloon owner is dead."

"There's still a lot of doubts in my mind, Siringo. As they've caught Butch Wicker. Maybe there won't be any more killings . . ."

"I wouldn't bet my life on it."

"Danny . . . do you feel his life is in danger, Mr. Siringo?"

"If Webb is still floating around it is." Charlie Siringo swung into the saddle. "Miss Tremane, your finding that list of names could possibly keep Danny Bellcone alive. I'll try to find Bellcone. Meanwhile, Mr. Mason, and Melissa, I just hope your father comes out of that coma . . . gives you some straight answers. Maybe he isn't involved in this after all. But the signs sure point that way." He swung the bronc around the corrals and sought the outward-running lane.

Only when the Pinkerton operative had passed out of view did Sid Mason break the heavy silence. "Melissa, he could be right as rain about your father."

"But . . . why?"

"It goes back to when you were born. You won't want to hear what I'm about to say, but so help me, its the truth. Len, here, you'd better tag along."

"You gonna tell Melissa about Salt Lake?"

"And a lot of other things. Afterward you might hate both your father and me, but I figure I've got no other choice in the matter."

"Supposing," she said desperately, "this Wicker is

the killer . . . and . . . and my father had nothing to do with this?"

"Lord, Lord," Sid Mason murmured sadly, "then all of our prayers and questions would be answered. But now it's time to clear the air."

Chapter Fifteen

Around the middle of the afternoon Sheriff Ben Taylor decided to send one of his deputies up to Tanner's Corner. Hammering at him had been Siringo's bold statement that Butch Wicker might not be the killer. He hated to think otherwise. Didn't want to believe the real killer was still floating about in the valley.

Last night he had bunked down at the jail, and then around three in the morning he'd been relieved by Mel Stern. Going home, Taylor had spent the remainder of the night camped out on a sofa in his living room, had left around six to head downtown again and to a cafe where the coffee they served could jolt a mule. During the day the sheriff and his deputies had kept watch over the jail and prowled among the many saloons and gaming joints. Everywhere they went was the angry talk of many wanting to get at Butch Wicker. This brought the sober-minded retort from Taylor to his deputies that Wicker should be taken up to Bozeman.

For a while the sun was a red lingering slash above the Tobacco Roots, just seeming to hang there as if to taunt Ben Taylor. He passed up supper in favor of idling at the jail, and because of an uneasy stomach. Troubling him at the moment was that nobody seemed to be going home for supper, the saloons being packed, and some business places that generally closed at six o'clock still open. Maybe everyone knew something he didn't. And again, maybe somebody could tell him why Charlie Siringo wasn't around to taunt him with more criminal logic.

"When this term expires, Mel, that's it."

"You've said that before."

"Before I was never faced with a bunch of folks getting murdered."

"What if Reese brings back word that Wicker *was* up at Tanner's Corner when Old Anse was murdered."

"The way everyone's talking, our releasing Wicker will be the same as signing his death warrant. Any coffee left?"

"Just some grounds." Deputy Mel Stern began rinsing out the coffee pot. "Better make another pot as this is going to be a long night."

"Where's Riggitt?"

"Making his rounds."

"Should have been back by now," growled the sheriff. "Here, I'll tend to making coffee. You'd better get out there and see what's going on."

The trouble with Deputy Sheriff Tom Riggitt

was that he couldn't let go of this growing anger he felt toward Butch Wicker. In the last three days, or ever since Wicker had been captured, most of the talk was of avenging the deaths of Doc Kreuger and Old Anse. Barely mentioned had been muleskinner, Jim Hardesty, the second man to die. It was as though Hardesty wasn't important enough to talk about, that he hadn't been around the valley long enough to count for much. But forgotten by most was that Jim Hardesty had married Deputy Riggitt's sister, Angeline. He'd been a good provider and a man of quiet conviction, and had gained Tom Riggitt's grudging respect.

He liked working for Ben Taylor, who'd taught his deputies to respect that badge they wore, though sometimes he felt the sheriff threaded too lightly around some of the town leaders. Pausing upon crossing a narrow intersection, Tom Riggitt drifted into shadow cast by an overhanging porch. Just past the porch and the other side of two tethered horses he could make out the portly form of P.J. Almond, a local merchant, having words with four others. Their cynical words drifted back to Deputy Riggitt, mostly of how they would deal with Butch Wicker.

Abruptly, Tom Riggitt swung back and passed around the corner and down a side street. He passed a couple of buildings, the grange hall, but approaching Sawyer's Bar, instead of making for the batwings he cut through an empty lot and entered by a side door.

"Glad you could make it, Tom."

He nodded at one of the men standing guard in

the dark hallway. "Are the others here yet?"

"Most of them."

Riggitt let himself into a large back room, the main piece of furniture being the felt-covered poker table and several chairs. The two lamps had their wicks turned low as befitting the guarded looks those already seated cast the newcomer. Claiming a chair but turning it around and drawing it away from the table some, he sat down. It still hadn't firmed in Riggitt's mind as to a final decision regarding this meeting. Last night he'd been here too, after midnight and until around three. Then it had all been talk of how these men wanted to form a vigilante committee. Such as what was going on up at Virginia City.

Most persuasive in this endeavor had been Raleigh Akins, one of the ringleaders and chief spokesman, whose honeyed Georgia voice had cut short a lot of arguments, and now Akins laid smiling eyes upon Tom Riggitt.

"Justice, as I stated last night, can be served in many ways, Tom."

"You did mention that," Riggitt grimaced, as he took a glass held out to him by Frank Rearden, a muleskinner. Then Riggitt drank sparingly of the whiskey as two more men shouldered into the room and claimed chairs.

"Everyone seems to be here," went on Akins. He had light, mottled skin, and with a cheroot held between two fingers of his hands clasped on the table top. Once upon a time a gambler, he'd started up a haberdashery shop here in Ennis. But Akins still gambled a lot, drank more, and according to rumor had just gotten married a third time. It was his vices more than his business acumen which had gained Akins a certain deal of respect, and he said, "After you cut out last night, Tom, the members of this committee voted, overwhelmingly, I might add, to see that justice is done. Your throwing in with us will make things a lot easier."

"I expect so, as you don't want me or anyone else blasting away with a scattergun when you boys show up."

"We don't want the sheriff or any of his deputies getting hurt."

Deputy Riggitt stared ponderingly at Akins dressed elegantly in a claw-hammer coat and boiled white shirt, went to the questioning eyes of others. Last night they had played upon the fact it had been his brother-in-law who'd been murdered. To inflame an anger that wouldn't go away. Maybe he could take the play away from these men by simply heading over to the jail and taking Wicker out back armed with a holstered sixgun, let quickness of draw decide the issue. In any case Tom Riggitt realized that if he threw in his lot with these vigilantes, his days as a lawman were over. But what the hell, he was single and not yet thirty, and over in that jail was a man everyone wanted dead. He held out his empty glass, to have Frank Rearden spill amber-tinted whiskey into it.

"Count me in," he finally said. "But now listen up, all of you. Reese should be back to stand the midnight watch."

"You never did tell us why the sheriff sent Reese

up to Tanner's Corner?"

"Some half-cocked notion that Wicker didn't do these killings."

Raleigh Akins laughed, said, "Perhaps it's time Ben Taylor called it quits."

"As I just said," Riggitts said loudly, "One thing Reese likes is going over and seeing that yeller-haired woman living out by Piedmont Street. So I figure I won't have no trouble taking over Reese's watch. But you make sure it's me in there before you come bustin' in."

The sheriff had just lost five games running to Deputy Mel Stern, a fact which displeased him greatly. He slapped his cards down and rubbed a tired hand across his eyes. "This is not my game."

"Never been this lucky before."

"Where the hell's Reese. Should have been back long before this." Ben Taylor's spur chinked dully when he swung his leg off the other chair, shoved up from behind his desk, took a long stride that brought him peering back into the cellblock. He could make out Butch Wicker's large frame draped under the covering blankets. He could feel his stomach rumbling, and the need for coffee other than Stern's pricking at his taste buds. "You're a Godawful cook, Mr. Stern."

"Ain't laid claim to be one."

"Could it be," he frowned, "that Mr. Reese has detoured over to see that widow woman?"

"Possible."

"Let's see, Reese has the midnight watch; going

on a quarter past eleven." He edged around his desk and reached for his hat hanging alongside Stern's on wall pegs. "If Reese don't get back, one of us will have to be here."

"I might as well do it, Ben, as it'll give me a chance to enjoy some more of my java."

"You must have a lead-lined belly, Mr. Stern. Think I'll chow down at the Old Tyme. Be back directly."

"Thought you was feudin' with that waitress over there, Emma . . ."

"Even Emma gets a night off." He moved to stand in the open doorway, and from there to swing his eyes up and down the long street. "Town's quieted down a lot, Mel. But don't let anybody in unless he's dripping bullets holes or it's Reese." He left a reassuring smile behind for his deputy.

Sheriff Ben Taylor knew this town and valley better'n most. Back before gold was discovered up in the Tobacco Roots, it was a place casting wary eyes at strangers. You pretty much knew everyone's pedigree, who could be counted on and those with quicksand for bottoms. He liked to think this town hadn't changed all that much. But it had, and he knew it. Ambling along downstreet, he passed men with faces he couldn't put names to, and even some of the newer business places were owned by Johnny-come-latelies. And speaking of newcomers, he mused, isn't that Charlie Siringo astride that bronc?

They spotted one another about the same time, Siringo reining over and looking down at Sheriff

Taylor, tired and trail-dusted, yet from the glint in his eyes he'd been on his way over to the jail. The sheriff said, "A cup of coffee won't hurt either of us. Where you been, Siringo?"

"What I'm hired to do," he replied as he tied up his horse and stepped up onto boardwalk.

"Bothering people, I reckon." He fell into step with the Pinkerton operative, but from force of habit glancing into the front windows of the saloons they passed, and with Siringo doing likewise.

"Town's quieted down."

"Could be everyone wanting to lynch Wicker"—the sheriff swung the screen door open and went ahead into the cafe—"are three sheets to the wind by now." The booth seat he eased onto faced the front door with Charlie Siringo sitting down opposite.

As the only waitress came over, Siringo said softly, "I went out to the Double Tree. Yes, coffee." He waited until their cups had been filled. "Had an interesting chat with Melissa Tremane . . . and Sid Mason. Found out more about that list she rode in to see you about, sheriff."

"How's Joshua Tremane?"

"Bad off—guess he won't last too much longer."

The sheriff speared Charlie Siringo with hard eyes. "Only reason you went out there, I expect, was that you've got suspicions about Tremane."

"I was hoping that's all they were." Siringo's gaze didn't waver as he added, "Locked up in Joshua Tremane's safe is a book in which some names are listed—Doc Kreuger's, Pickard's, Sid Mason's . . . and a muleskinner named Bellcone.

There's another name in there too, Ben, a J. Brown, and that Tremane has been paying this hombre."

Ben Taylor blinked away some of his skepticism as he sipped from his cup. At that moment he felt a lot older. He let play through his mind the way rancher, Joshua Tremane had operated in the past. For certain the man played for keeps, always liked to come out top dog in anything. "Old Anse, he used to work for the Double Tree, as does Mason now. Kreuger's name being there does get me to thinking, Siringo. The fact the man got killed. But where does the Bellcone's fit in?"

"As you recall, Tremane's daughter was sweet on Danny Bellcone. And friends of Bellcone's busted those church windows."

"Tremane was always overly protective of Melissa. But to want Bellcone done in? Don't make sense."

"It does if you remember Tremane's true character. The answer to these killings can be found out at the Double Tree. Not with Tremane or his daughter. But with Sid Mason. Mason was there from the beginning. Which is probably why Tremane wants him gunned down. I've got the feeling, Ben, this has something to do with Tremane's daughter."

"Damnit, Siringo, you're talking like a blind man clinging to a wall." He swept a disturbed glance over at Deputy Mel Stern looming in the open doorway, and Taylor barked out, "So Reese finally got back."

"Nope, it was Tom Riggitt coming over to relieve

me, Ben. Reese got an awful late start up to Tanner's Corner; figure he decided to overnight."

"Come morning," said Siringo, "we'll find out that Wicker just might not have killed anyone."

"Meaning it's going to be another long night," the sheriff said grumpily as the waitress arrived with his food. He looked at Stern dragging a chair over and back at Siringo. "As I said earlier today, this is my last go-around as a lawman. 'Cause this job can wreck a man's stomach faster'n anything."

By one o'clock the town had quieted into its usual peacefulness, meaning that a few all-night poker sessions were still going on but most of the saloons were emptied out. As always there were a few stragglers draping solitary shadows along Main Street and the occasional clop-clopping of a rider pointing his bronc homeward. About the only item of particular interest was a fistfight that had just broken up behind the Moonlight Saloon, a muleskinner coming out about even with a cowhand. Now these men found their way to nearby shelter or home, the progress of some of these men watched by Deputy Tom Riggitt.

The sheriff had stopped by just after midnight to say he was going home, and that Mel Stern would come in around four. To while away his uncertainties Deputy Riggitt started playing solitaire, found that he couldn't get his mind set right on the game, then tried flipping cards into his hat perched on a chair. More often he would shove up abruptly and look out a window or the door for those he knew were coming.

Up in his room in a boarding house, lawman Mel Stern was relaxing over a bottle of corn liquor. Usually his limit was no more'n two shots, but tonight he was pondering over the day's happenings while refilling his shot glass a third time. What he couldn't figure out was Tom Riggitt coming in, since Riggitt often voiced his displeasure at having to work at night.

Still awake in the bedroom of his home was Sheriff Ben Taylor, though he lay in bed beside his wife just settling back into sleep. Occupying his thoughts was the reappearance of Charlie Siringo, who'd brought in some awful disturbing news as to Tremane being involved in these killings. The more he mulled over Butch Wicker being the killer, the more Ben Taylor began to believe the man was locked up unjustly. In every instance witnesses to these killings had stated only one shot had been fired, and from a considerable distance. Wicker may tote a .50 caliber rifle, but as Siringo had told him, to kill at such a distance a man needed a scope. "If not Wicker, then who?"

In his hotel room Charlie Siringo stood looking out a window. He felt restless, curiously remote. Though he'd unbuckled his gunbelt and shucked his hat and leather coat, he still wore trailworn clothing. Somewhere in town, he felt, was the real killer. Probably sleeping peaceable at the moment, and unconcerned about Butch Wicker being locked up. If he'd gotten in earlier, he would have gone to the post office in case the Denver office had mailed him new instructions or over to the telegraph office. It could be that the far-flung Pinkerton network had come up with the killer's name. This would at least give him something to focus on, take this worried edge away. There was still a lot of night left. A time when the pack liked to take the law into their own hands. And there was little doubt in Charlie Siringo's mind that there'd be an attempt to get at the buffalo hunter. Maybe later tonight, when the moon had set and the coyotes and wolves no longer yowled their lonesome calls, and when the shadows seemed darkest.

"Can't sleep," he complained. "Just can't seem to shake the feeling something's gonna happen tonight." Turning, he stepped over to the washstand to dip his hands into the wash basin and splash cold water over his face. He hadn't shaved for a couple of days and what he saw in the wall mirror were the tired eyes of a middle-aged man, the stubble a bluish-black, and the thin, lanky face crowned by a full head of black hair. He dried his face with a towel he'd used before, while striding back to the window and staring down the black ribbon of Main Street. "If anything happens, it'll come later, as I said when the moon is down." Turning out the lamp, he draped his clothed body on the bed, for Siringo had decided to catnap for an hour before rising and looking in on deputy sheriff Tom Riggitt and his prisoner.

They began quartering in from all sections of Ennis, keeping to the alleys instead of the streets, and beelining for the corrals out back of the

Hoaglund Freighting Company. A few dogs picked up their movements and began barking; other than that it was quiet. At twenty minutes after two a command was given by one of the ringleaders to move out. And then they did, in two bunches. But not separating until after they reached the hanging grounds, a livery stable on Clark Street, where almost of their own volition vengeful eyes turned to look upward at a pulley and the rope dangling from a crossbeam used to lift hay into the loft. But the rope they'd used on Wicker lay coiled over the shoulder of a muleskinner, who broke to move with others into an alleyway running toward Main Street.

Out on Main Street, they fanned out, were guided across the wide and rock-hard expanse of street by a lonely arm of light coming out of a jail window. They carried no rifles, just sidearms, and their unyielding anger. Only when a cautious rapping at the door caused it to be unlocked and swung open by Deputy Riggitt were torches lighted. In the flickering light cast by the torches every face was revealed, with all of them seeming to be cast from the same lusting mold, the eyes shining with killing expectancy.

When four men unlocked Butch Wicker's cell and stormed in, he came awake with a wild yell, but with further resistance quietened by a blow from a gun butt to his head. They picked their prey up as one would a mule deer just run down and killed, one man to a limb and carrying him out shoulder-high. Out in the street, others reached to help carry the buffalo hunter at a quickened pace back upstreet as the rest of the would-be vigilantes poured away from the back of the jail and out into the street to trail behind, talking now and laughing in nervous undertones.

As the last of the vigilantes spilled off the street into an alleyway, up in his hotel room Charlie Siringo jerked an eye open, fought to unpry the other eye while trying to focus them. What had wakened him? Yes, something bright flickering against the window panes. Struggling up from the bed, he stepped over to the window. His eyes swept northward along the street, to the location of the jail and beyond. Then off to the left he spotted the last of the mob spilling into an alley, the light from their torches leaving a damning halo behind, and he knew they'd gotten to Butch Wicker.

Spinning away from the window, Charlie Siringo grabbed his sombrero and holstered gun hanging from the bed frame, shoved the hat over his head as he bolted out of the room to take the staircase two steps at a time. He rushed out into the street as he buckled the gunbelt around his waist. Then as he broke running toward the jail, Siringo palmed his Colt's and fired three shots into the dark, star-studded sky.

Siringo was still holding his Colt's when he shouldered into the jail office. On the floor and with blood staining the side of his head lay a deputy, the barred door to the cellblock standing open, and without going back there Siringo knew the buffalo hunter was gone.

"Taken out to be hung."

He hurried outside and crossed over to hurry down the alley. Emerging from it, he broke stride to stare in bitter dismay at Butch Wicker's body swaying high above the ground. Still clustered around were the men responsible for hanging the buffalo hunter. Siringo could have gone in and accosted them, realized it would do no good at this point in time. For all intents and purposes the fine citizens of Ennis believed they had just hung a vicious killer. They all believe these killings are over now, he mused bitterly. They will be if I catch the real killer. Then the truth will come out. He turned to trudge back up the alley.

As he'd expected, his firing his sixgun had brought the other lawmen of Madison County to the jail. He was halfway across the street when Sheriff Ben Taylor rushed outside and slowed his pace, and to say to Siringo, "You fire them shots?"

"Yup, Ben, but it's too late."

"Damn, I should have been here."

"Maybe," Charlie Siringo replied. "One thing I noticed . . ."

"Yeah?"

"They didn't have to break in and get at Wicker."

"Yeah, the door hadn't been busted in?" Ben Taylor's lips pursed in anger. "Riggitt . . . must have just let them in."

"Or maybe he didn't want to get hurt."

"Should have taken this into consideration, Siringo . . . and that is that Tom Riggitt's sister was married to that muleskinner who got killed.

Guess I should have heeded my own counsel and brought my prisoner up to Bozeman for safekeeping. You still . . . you still think Wicker isn't the killer . . . ?"

"Come morning your deputy should be back."

"Yup," he said with an explosion of wondering air, "an' I just hope you're wrong, Mr. Siringo."

Chapter Sixteen

Even after the sun had struck over the eastern peaks Sheriff Ben Taylor still carried within him the forlorn hope Butch Wicker had been guilty of the charges brought against him. It had been Taylor and Stern, and Charlie Siringo going over and cutting down Wicker's body. They'd taken the body over to Turner's Funeral Home, with the sheriff telling the undertaker all expenses would be picked up by the county. A pine box would do, and there'd be no church services.

Now that it was over, he'd anticipated Charlie Siringo heading back to Denver, only to be painfully reminded by Siringo—the deputy he'd sent up to Tanner's Corner should be showing up at any time. That had been during the dying fragments of the night. At which time they'd gone their separate ways, Siringo, the sheriff supposed, back to his hotel, but for Ben Taylor a lonely walk over to his jail. When he'd gotten there, Tom Riggitt was gone, but there on his desk lay Riggitt's deputy sheriff's badge.

"Figured Riggitt was in on it."

Dropping the badge in a desk drawer, Taylor got the fire going in the potbellied stove, made a fresh pot of coffee. Slumping into a chair behind his desk, he tried rehashing over the events of the past few weeks. Had he acted properly as the sheriff of Madison County? At the very least he should have insisted the county hire more deputies. Like everyone else, he felt a lot better when Wicker had been arrested. Ennis's only newspaper had proclaimed this in bold headlines, made Ben Taylor out to be some kind of hero. But all the while, there was Charlie Siringo insisting Butch Wicker wasn't the killer.

Sadly he murmured, "Wicker's dead . . . and I guess that's the way it was meant to be."

He lingered in his office as the sun climbed higher to spear the windows with a yellowy glare. And as it warmed up, he opened the front door to let in fresh air. There, he looked out at a lot of familiar faces, some folks opening their places of business, more of them coming downtown to catch the latest news, which of course was last night's hanging. For some reason Ben Taylor felt like an outsider, this bitter feeling over what had happened adding coal to the fire burning inside him. Those he saw had smiles, seemed to walk more boldly, and in a way he couldn't blame them. Recriminations would come later, that is, if what Siringo kept telling him was true.

It was then he sensed rather than saw the deputy he'd sent up to Tanner's Corner jog his bronc onto Main Street from the connecting stagecoach road, and Ben Taylor's eyes swiveled upstreet. Coming in was a long line of freight wagons scudding out dust, then through and past this dustiness came Deputy Sheriff Cal Reese, this at a fast canter. Reluctantly the sheriff stepped onto the boardwalk. Coming up, Reese didn't swing down but sat there, and Ben Taylor found himself blurting out, "Was he up there? Was Wicker up there when Doc Kreuger was killed?"

"He was," the deputy said flatly.

"For how long?"

"According to eyewitnesses, Butch Wicker rode in to Tanner's Corner two days before the first killing. Didn't make tracks outta there for at least a week." Concern for the man he worked for flared in Cal Reese's eyes when the sheriff grasped the hitching rack post so hard his knuckles whitened. "Something happen here?"

It was as if Ben Taylor hadn't heard Reese's last words. For he seemed to stare blindly downstreet, and with pain lines etched in the sheriff's face. He swung away, then checked himself and threw back at his deputy, "They broke in last night and took Wicker; strung him up."

"I should have got back sooner. I . . . I'm sorry, Ben . . ."

"Isn't your fault, Cal. All mine."

"What do we do now?" But Reese asked the sheriff that as he was going into his office. Then as he swung down, Ben Taylor emerged wearing his hat.

"Tie up that bronc and come with me."

It took the lawmen exactly two minutes to tramp

along the boardwalk and hurry into the Cattlemen's Hotel, less time than that to take the staircase and to have the sheriff shove into Charlie Siringo's room. Siringo, surprise widening his eyes, gazed up from the letter he had been reading. He gazed past the sheriff at Cal Reese. Then he pushed up from the chair and said, "You must be Reese."

"Damn, you were right all along."

"I wish it were otherwise, Ben."

"Whoever's doing these killings must sure be laughin' right about now. Who, Siringo, you got any idea?"

"Sharpshooter's name is Adin Webb; according to this letter." He passed it to the sheriff. "We found this out, compliments of a saloon owner down in Waco. Seems this saloon owner wanted to bare his soul, before a priest down there performed last rites."

"Not much of a description to go on, Siringo."

"Sooner or later Webb'll make a mistake."

"It can't be any bigger than those who broke Wicker out and strung him up," the sheriff said bitterly. "What about this other thing you've been jawing on . . . that Joshua Tremane brought this sharpshooter in here . . ."

"You've had time to think on it, Ben. Webb charges a heap just for killing one man. Who other than rancher Tremane could afford paying what Webb is asking? And . . . there's the list of names belonging to Tremane."

"I hate to admit it, Siringo, even think it. That Tremane is behind this. But you were right about

Wicker. Meanwhile"—he removed his sweat-stained hat and let his hand drop to his side—"I figure we keep this to ourselves. For the time being we'll let everyone believe Wicker was the murderer. As you said, Charlie Siringo, and I believe now too, two other men are earmarked for death—Sid Mason and this Bellcone kid."

"The Bellcones," said Reese, "left with their wagons for the Tobacco Roots late last week."

"Means they'll be back in a day or two," pondered Taylor. "But the best thing I can do right now is ride out to the Double Tree and find out what I can from Sid Mason. And, Siringo, I'm ordering my deputies to help you find the killer. What really gets to me is that Webb was staying here all the time . . . going out to do his killings . . . heading back in again."

"Trouble is," said Charlie Siringo, "there are a lot around here drifted up from the south. So Webb coming from Missouri means he'll fit right in."

With the sheriff leaving for the Double Tree ranch, Charlie Siringo and Deputy Marshals Stern and Reese scattered around to the hotels and boarding houses in their search for the man from Taney County. Little did they realize that a man clothed in houndstooth check was urging his packhorse onto one of the lanes passing out into the Madison Valley.

Yesterday Adin Webb had staged down from Bozeman. After learning this morning of Butch Wicker being lynched, Webb had shrugged this off as an unfortunate circumstance. Riding out now, he was more relaxed than he'd been since coming here. The sun-dappled sky spiked with ribbons of high clouds seemed a little friendlier, and more importantly to Webb, once he got rid of Danny Bellcone there was only one more man to kill.

"Maybe I should cut out now," he said to his horse jogging around a washed out part of the lane passing through a marshy area. Knowing he wouldn't, however, Adin Webb smiled when he thought about the extra money he'd be getting, with his teeth clamping down harder on a piece of licorice rock candy.

"Southern gentleman, you say?" The manager of Ennis's Courtland Hotel said to Deputy Sheriff Mel Stern and Charlie Siringo. One of the day clerks stood nearby. And at four in the afternoon they were the only ones in the lobby, the diamond-shaped clock behind the counter just sounding the hour. "People come and go . . . rarely stay for any length of time."

"We do have some regulars; folks staying year-round."

Siringo looked at the clerk. "The man we're looking for could have checked in within the last month. He wouldn't be a miner or roughneck . . . probably be posing as a carpetbagger."

"There is our botanist."

"Yes," the clerk agreed somewhat reluctantly, "Mr. L.C. Phillips. Arrived about a month ago."

"Didn't Mr. Phillips," the manager said thoughtfully, "have special locks made for one of the dressers in his room? Well, Bentley?"

"Yessir, he did." The clerk shifted uneasily. "He . . . Mr. Phillips paid me to keep quiet about this."

"The key to his room," demanded Deputy Mel Stern.

"It would please us greatly," said Charlie Siringo as the deputy was handed a key, "that you go about your business." Then the manager left hurriedly to go into his office as Siringo and Mel Stern crossed to the staircase, where Siringo said quietly, "Most likely Phillips isn't in his room. But no sense taking any chances." He went first up the creaking staircase, to turn left on the worn carpeting of a second floor corridor. He felt no need at this point to unlimber his sixgun, though easing it clear of leather and back again while moving up to the closed door of Room 225. Mimicking as close as he could the day clerk's reedy voice, he said while rapping tentatively, "Mr. Phillips, I've a message for you."

Behind Siringo, the deputy sheriff had eased out his handgun, and when Siringo rattled the panes again, Stern said, "Most likely he's out someplace."

Unlocking the door, Charlie Siringo went in first, and without bothering to palm his weapon. The bed was made, the shades up, and through an open closet door he could see a valise on the floor and items of clothing draped from hangers. In one corner in an earthen vase had been planted a greenleafed fern, which caused Siringo to remark, "For someone claiming to be a plant expert its awful strange that plant squats in a dark corner and out of sunlight."

By way of easing the tension Mel Stern remarked, "Maybe it's taking a nap."

A wry smile breaking across his mouth, Siringo said, "I'll try this dresser first." Reaching into a trouser pocket, he took out a knife and pulled out a blade while pulling out dresser drawers, with only the bottom drawer refusing to open. Kneeling, he murmured, "Wood's been reworked and varnished and a new lock put in."

As Charlie Siringo grasped both metal drawer handles and tried to force the drawer open, the deputy said, "I believe this is called breaking and entering. Need a hand?"

"Nope," grunted Siringo as the lock broke and the drawer sprang open. He had fallen back, and now he regained his balance along with lifting up the drawer and setting it on the bed. Both men viewed the large dark blue cloth covering the contents of the drawer. Lifting this aside, Siringo as did Mel Stern stared at the implements used by a rifleman. There was a can of Dupont powder, a powder measuring thimble, some spare cylinders holding what appeared to be caliber .50 leaden balls, and with beeswax sealing the cylinders. The largest item contained in the drawer was a bullet mold, with sprue cutting pincher handles. Lastly, and this Siringo picked up, a scale used to weigh gold.

"This Mr. Phillips knows his business."

"For certain he isn't any botanist."

"Every ball he makes he weighs on this scale so

there'll be no variance. Man's a professional."

"And our killer."

"The thought gives me little comfort."

"Yes," agreed Stern, "after what they done to Butch Wicker. The sheriff, Ben left for the Double Tree. Which leaves us to arrest this backshooting hombre."

"Could be our Mr. Adin Webb, aka L.C. Phillips, left too."

"To . . . try and waylay Danny Bellcone . . ."

"Yup," Charlie Siringo said. "But going easy as he probably figures as does everyone else around here that we've closed the case on these killings."

"You know, Charlie, once the truth comes out, this is going to be a hard place to live at. A shameful thing Wicker had to die this way."

They went out into the hallway, with Siringo saying, "At the time they thought they were right. Even if we arrest Adin Webb there'll be a lot of folks still believing that Wicker was the killer. You said earlier the Bellcones should be coming back from Virginia City."

"Same as always, Charlie, about two weeks to make a roundtrip up there and back."

Out in front of the hotel, Deputy Mel Stern nodded as the Pinkerton operative said they should meet at the Clark Street livery stable within the half-hour.

"I'll have Reese there and our horses saddled. This Adin Webb, he's a sly one."

"And out there someplace," Charlie Siringo threw back as he hurried toward his downstreet hotel and his rifle and the bedroll he'd take along.

He felt an easing of tension now that they'd found tangible evidence of the sharpshooter's presence. He knew without question had Webb come up here to kill just one man, there'd still be no clues to his identity. What had held the man from Taney County here, greed, pride in his work, or could it be, pondered Siringo, the man simply liked to kill? In a way Webb was like a lobo wolf, one of those cast out by the pack and having to rely on his own skills and cunning to survive.

"Wolfine of character, probably. And with no conscience to still this killing lust."

Short of the half-hour by ten minutes the lawmen and Charlie Siringo headed westward into the searing flames of the afternoon sun.

Chapter Seventeen

On the way out here Ben Taylor had tried to argue himself into thinking that the charges brought by this Pinkerton operative against the owner of the Double Tree were akin to false dawn, having no validity to them. After all, Joshua Tremane had done a lot of good for the valley and Ennis. Those who envied the rancher called him a land grabber, and a lot of other names one wouldn't repeat in church.

Now to some facts, as presented to him by Charlie Siringo. Seven years ago two ranchers had died under mysterious circumstances, and with Tremane profiting from their deaths. Like these recent murders, the weapon used had been of a .50 caliber or maybe larger. Rubbing against what Siringo had laid out was Tremane hiring this buffalo hunter. By reputation Butch Wicker couldn't even be trusted to button up his own fly, as he'd had a wandering mind. And knowing Tremane, the rancher would only hire top-notchers, be it waddies for his Double Tree spread or business associates.

"What galls me is Siringo still insisting Butch Wicker isn't the killer."

A sour grimace matching the irritated glint in his eyes, Sheriff Ben Taylor headed in toward the main buildings on a lane familiar to him. In his early years as sheriff it was customary for him to come out here at Tremane's invite. That was before Tremane's daughter had been born. In the years afterward such invitations were seldom extended to him or others Joshua Tremane called friends.

Coming out from the corrals as Ben Taylor eased in was segundo Ozzie Browning. He didn't care too much for Browning as the man was somewhat of a bully, but civilly he said, "How do, Ozzie."

"Something I can help you with?"

"That depends." He made no attempt to dismount as he gazed into Ozzie Browning's unfriendly eyes. The ranch foreman had on chaps but no gunbelt, and he stood with his legs spread apart in a poise of arrogant defiance. This got to the sheriff, as had his having to come out here and confront a man rumored to be dying. "Sid Mason around?"

"Anything you have to say to Mason you can say to me, Taylor."

"I never did like you, Ozzie," he said somberly. "It still puzzles me deeply, Tremane making you his foreman."

Browning unhooked his large, meaty hands from

his belt and shaped one into a half-raised fist as he muttered angrily, "I don't know why you're on the prod, Taylor, but you're on my territory now."

"Your stomping grounds would be a better way of saying it."

"What the hell's that supposed to mean?"

"You did a helluva job beating up on Danny Bellcone."

"I wasn't there, damn you."

"That isn't the way I hear it."

Ozzie Browning came around to the side of the horse with the intentions of pulling the sheriff out of the saddle. But checked up short when he found himself staring into the muzzle of Ben Taylor's Peacemaker, then drew back farther when Taylor thumbed the hammer back and said peaceably, "By rights I should charge you with assault and battery."

"But I didn't do nothing," he blustered.

"I consider your presence a criminal offense." He swiveled the barrel of his sixgun at a hiproofed barn backgrounding the corrals. "Should be a fork in there . . . and a wheelbarrow."

"Should be," Browning found himself saying.

"And a lot of horse turds that need to be forked out of the runways."

"Why . . . damn you, Taylor, I'll . . ."

"You'll tend to that chore or I just might bust the heels off those fancy Justins you're wearing. That's it, keep trotting that way . . ." As Ben Taylor eased the hammer down on his Peacemaker the sight of Sid Mason moving down a walkway eased some of his anger. Still asaddle, he brought his horse over to a gate in the stone fence hemming in the spacious ranchhouse, and here he swung down.

"Ben, we were just talking about you . . . Melissa and I were, that is. You haven't been out here since . . . by golly, last fall." He grasped the sheriff's outstretched hand.

Ben Taylor said, "It was more like two years ago. How is Joshua?"

"Failing. Still in a coma. Well, come on in. Coffee's on."

The sheriff left his horse tied to the gate and followed Sid Mason into the front hallway, where he wiped his boots on a large braided rug, left his hat dangling on a wall peg. In the front living room, and with Mason standing to one side, he smiled at the daughter of Joshua Tremane sitting at the long, polished table. Melissa Tremane had her hands folded before her, a handkerchief grasped in them, and to Ben Taylor's estimation a strange and haunted expression on her face, and her eyes seemed sort of redrimmed.

"Sheriff, how delightful to see you."

"Been a long time. My, how you've grown. Can I take the liberty of still calling you Melissa?"

"Please, Ben, sit down."

He folded onto a chair as did Sid Mason. Coffee and a light repast of meats, beef, turkey, prairie chicken, and other foods grown out here at the Double Tree, was spread out on the table by a servant. Then the three of them were left with their uncertain thoughts. In a questioning voice Ben

Taylor brought up Melissa's coming in to see him a short time ago. "You mentioned a list? One you'd found among your father's papers?"

She set her fork on her plate and looked to Sid Mason for support, who said, "I know you love your father. But I probably know him a lot better than you do. I know that Joshua is capable of many things. But"—Mason's eyes swept to the sheriff—"coldblooded murder?"

Now Melissa Tremane found her voice. "Is that why you came out, Ben? To accuse my father of . . . of complicity in these murders?"

"Truly," he replied, "I don't know what to believe. If you remember, you came to me . . ."

"Yes, I did." She rubbed her forearm; a worried gesture. "We . . . Sid and I, discussed it."

Nodding, Ben Taylor said, "Your father's been sick—which could account for any uncharacteristic actions on his part." He reached for his cup, brought his hand away, groped for something to say. "These killings; can't find anything to tie them together."

"If, Ben, my father is involved," she said, "I know the reason why."

"No," protested Sid Mason, "you mustn't . . ."

"But I must," Melissa Tremane said sharply. "Ben, it all goes back to when I was born." Whereupon the daughter of Joshua Tremane told plainly of how she came to be born westward in Utah. When she had finished, she reached out and laid her hand over Sid Mason's. "As you told me before, Sid, the truth must come out."

"Must it!"

The rasping voice of Joshua Tremane came striking out at them from a back hallway, and as one they swung to stare at him standing on his crutches, a thinned out skeleton of a man, with his unkempt and gray hair flayed out as if the wind were picking at it, and swaying now against the wall, yet still able to hold onto a small caliber revolver. Dark blue pajamas were draped loosely over his wasted frame, and he was barefooted. His eyes, sunken as they were in their sockets, had in them a crazed glare. He speared them at Sid Mason.

"Ozzie, you did deposit that money up to Bozeman . . . for that damned Webb. Did he kill Bellcone yet? Damnit, Ozzie, answer me."

The scream piercing out of Melissa Tremane brought her father's hesitant eyes swinging o her. Then he shrank back as a moment of lucidity came. And the awful realization that his part in the murders had been found out.

Rising, as did Sid Mason, the sheriff stepped away from the table and advanced on the rancher, and Taylor said, "Easy, Joshua, all we want is your gun . . . easy, now . . ."

"No," he said cruelly, and as madness shut the door on that brief instant of sanity, "you can't doublecross me this way, Browning." Joshua Tremane's shaking hand centered on his old friend, Mason, and with the unsteady finger crooking to spring back the trigger, Sheriff Ben Taylor in one smooth movement swept out his Peacemaker and et it detonate. The heavy slug tore into the rancher's chest to end his suffering. Again a sobbing scream came from his daughter as he simply folded to the floor.

"He gave me no choice," Ben said as his gun fell to his side.

Sid Mason went over and crouched by Melissa Tremane holding her father's hand. He pressed a hand against the rancher's neck, and murmured to her, "Joshua's dead. Maybe . . . maybe it's better this way." He helped her stand up.

Still held by the shock of seeing her father killed by a bullet from the sheriff's gun, Melissa stared with unseeing eyes at Ben Taylor, and now, shaking her head to clear it, she said, "That killer . . . is he still out there?"

"I reckon he is."

"Danny . . . you must warn him. And Sid . . . your name is on that list of my father's."

"All because Joshua felt he was protecting you," Sid Mason said. "Ben, you'd best try and warn Danny Bellcone. We'll see that Joshua gets a proper burial. In his way, he wasn't all that bad. But I guess it was more than his body being crippled by this disease."

"How deeply do you figure Ozzie Browning was involved in this?"

"I don't figure he had any idea Joshua Tremane was behind these killings."

"Suppose not," said Sheriff Ben Taylor as he holstered his sixgun on the way to the front door. "Sid, for now I want you staying close to this ranch. 'Cause once he guns down Bellcone, it'll be you he sights in on next."

"Any idea who it is?"

"A man a lot smarter than Butch Wicker . . . as Charlie Siringo kept telling me." Then the screen door slammed behind the sheriff trotting toward his waiting horse.

Chapter Eighteen

Danny Bellcone felt a lot better when they cleared the last stands of pine forest on the eastern slopes of the Tobacco Roots. Before it had started raining last night the muleskinners heard the reverberating echoes of distant gunfire. At the time they'd been clustered around their campfire pitched under sheltering pines, had broken for their rifles, only to have the hammering of guns stop as quickly as it had started. They all knew some innocent people had just been bushwhacked by highwaymen. Then the stars had been blotted out as a sudden gust of cold air heralded an approaching rainstorm.

Mud clung tenaciously to their wagon wheels and the mules found it hard going on the downsloping road. Though it had cleared, rainwater ran in thirsty and gouging rivulets across the narrow expanse of track. There was in the air the tangy scent of pine, with the Madison Valley opening up to them.

Danny's was the second wagon in a train of fifteen more. Customarily he'd be in the lead, but the right front wheel on his wagon had a couple of broken spokes and was wobbling, so Link Cavanaugh was up there. Despite the fact it paid good, he was getting to dislike this job of reining mules up into the mountains just to unload his cargo and make that long return journey to Ennis. What had firmed in his mind was Danny Bellcone's decision to sell his wagons and clear out of the valley. A deeper reason was his concern for his brother, Mickey, of Mickey's being exposed to the raw life up in the mining camps. Just last week he'd come upon his brother out in the pines by his lonesome and gurgling away at a bottle of corn whiskey. At the time he couldn't argue with Mickey Bellcone's bold statement that if he was considered to be a muleskinner he had a right to drink same as everyone else. All the same Danny had taken possession of the bottle.

"Guess Mickey's right," he mused, whereupon he called out to Cavanaugh and his fellow muleskinners, "We'll take a breather."

He simply reined up his mules on the road and set the brake before clambering down and crouching to cast worried eyes at the right front wheel. Erik Olsen meandered up to say, "It seems to be holding."

"If we take it easy it just might last."

Link Cavanaugh, uncorking his canteen, said, "Gonna be a hot one. Still it's awful misty down in the valley."

"A rain shower will do that."

"That was more than a rain shower. That one

bolt of lightning hit so close last night I swear I saw the Pearly Gates open."

The other muleskinners gathered around, some squatting under the few scattered trees, others to mosey over to a creek to the north. Soon everyone was back under the trees, and with everyone centering their thoughts upon the startling events taking place back in Ennis. For word had carried up to them in Virginia City of how Butch Wicker had been lynched. It was Erik Olsen breaking the silence.

"Never figured Wicker as being that way."

"Yup, mean as all get out—but just a blowhard."

"Well, he's bragging to the angels now."

"I still don't think Wicker did these killings."

"Come on, Danny, he's about the only one in these parts who packed a .50 caliber buffalo gun."

"Wicker deserved what he got."

As they tarried on the high mountainous road, the wind began picking up. It came out of the southwest, swept through the pine forest of the mountain, scudded hotly along the road to bake out its downsloping surface, and from there the wind dipped into the valley. The wind created updrafts near the foothills, where hawks could be seen as they caught the hot and upspiraling wind to ride it up past the muleskinners on motionless wings. Now the muleskinners scattered to their wagons to began the final leg of their journey into Ennis.

It took them the greater shank of the afternoon to wend down off the mountain. And it was coming onto sundown when they were finally approaching a small cluster of buildings sheltered by a few cottonwoods. Oftentimes they would overnight here at Leland Sawyer's place, drawing water from his well to water their stock and occasionally to use his forge to repair one of the wagons. They swept into a hollow to have the rancher come out of his log barn as his dogs began barking and darting toward the wagons. He returned Link Cavanaugh's wave and held there until the muleskinners had brought their wagons into ragged rows by the corrals. His practiced eye had taken in that wobbling wheel hooked to Danny Bellcone's wagon, and he moved that way.

"Seems you've got yourself a busted wheel, Danny."

"My fault—should have avoided some rocks up there."

"It'll happen." He bent over to place a calloused hand on a broken spoke. "These spokes are busted; some more cracked. Up here though, the rim's bent out of shape. First thing in the morning I'll heat up my forge."

"I appreciate that, Mr. Sawyer." Going back, Danny opened the tailgate on his high-sided freight wagon, and reaching in he lifted out a sack of flour and some canned food.

"Son, there's no need for that."

"Payment for fixin' that wheel."

"Suppose the flour would come in handy at that."

Later that evening those who'd arrived with the wagon train began settling into their bedrolls to the soothing notes of a muleskinner playing his harmonica. A lot of them had taken to sleeping in their wagons rather than on the ground as sidewinders liked to slither in and share the warmth of their bedrolls. Danny Bellcone and several others had found nighting places under their wagons. A couple of slow tunes later the muleskinner stopped playing his harmonica, and but for a couple of hound dogs snapping and baying at one another, a deep silence descended upon the encampment.

There came to Danny Bellcone, now that he was back in the Madison Valley, how it had felt to hold Melissa in his arms again. He couldn't deny that he wanted her, though he felt marriage was out of the question. She was above his station in life, something that he couldn't do anything about. And there was her father, a man, he felt, who couldn't forget nor forgive. Even if Joshua Tremane did pass away, the man's ghost would always be there to remind Danny of what the rancher had done to his family, and to him.

In the morning only Danny Bellcone remained at Leland Sawyer's small spreading of log buildings just south of the main freighting road. Though the rancher had started working on the busted wheel just after sunup, it wasn't until around ten o'clock on this windy morning that he was slipping the wheel onto the greased axle. Shortly thereafter he straightened up and smiled at Danny as he used an old rag to wipe the grease from his hands.

"Good as new."

Danny Bellcone proceeded to exchange a few pleasantries with the rancher before he headed the six mules hitched to his freight wagon out onto the lane. Late afternoon, by his reckoning, would bring him back to Ennis. Last night he'd firmed up his decision to sell his wagons and mules. And instead of making for the gold diggings as so many others were doing, he would work his way west, maybe getting in a little fishing along the way, and check out what was happening at that Butte copper mining town. Not so much to get work at the mines but to buy into some business, and get some schooling for his brother, which wouldn't set too good with Mickey. But with the inroads made by all of these settlers coming in, things were changing. Freighting such as he was doing would end once more railroad spur lines were built. And just maybe farther west he could let any thoughts of Melissa Tremane pass away.

"Just wasn't meant to be."

Just past a large cottonwood having been struck by lightning sometime ago but with a large branch that had been sheared away still dangling and almost touching the ground one of the deputy sheriffs jerked his head at a freight wagon touching over a hillock.

"Might be Bellcone's outfit."

They set their mounts into a canter. It had been cold last night, the cooler weather caused by the passing rainstorm, and forcing the lawmen into seeking shelter which proved out to be the hayloft of a barn. But in these parts a man never complained about having any kind of roof over his head. Along the way Charlie Siringo had inquired about the layout of the valley adjacent to the road, and as to places a man could set up an ambush. Plenty of them, he'd been told.

"Mel," Siringo said, and as the other wagons came into view, "seems they're coming along nice and easy."

"It's Bellcone's outfit all right as I recognize Cavanaugh driving the front wagon. Yup, if something had happened they'd still be circled up out there." He slowed into a walk. "How goes it, Link?"

"You boys just out exercising your hosses . . ."

"I don't see Danny Bellcone?"

"One of his wheels got busted; left him back at Sawyer's. He told us to go on ahead. What's up, Mel?"

Charlie Siringo answered for the deputy sheriff, "Nothing, we hope. Let's ride." Leaving a tight smile for Link Cavanaugh, Siringo swung away followed by Stern and Reese. Only when the wagons had fallen behind, and the others were riding abreast of him did Siringo say, "No sense bothering those muleskinners with detail."

"They sure threw us a lot of snake-eyed looks."

"What we don't want is that wagon train taking out after us. The sight of them coming back could spook that killing sharpshooter away."

"You think he's out here?"

"I know Webb is out here . . . some damned

place. Probably sighting in on Bellcone right about now. How far to Sawyer's place?"

"Not over fifteen miles."

"Far enough," said Charlie Siringo, and he stepped up the cantering pace of his horse.

The mules picked up on it first, that something was wrong. Perhaps that a predator was lurking close at hand. Knowing that sometimes highwaymen would come down to do their robbing work in the valley, Danny Bellcone kept scanning the heat-distorted reaches of valley floor. He was well past the few fringes of the foothills, and now out on a level area carpeted with waist-high bluestem and needle-grass bending in the wind. The prairie grass spread south for about a mile where a low butte reared up, while opposite the valley floor extended in an unbroken line some four miles where it began to flow upward.

He hadn't been all that concerned when the other wagons had pulled out this morning, as outlaws never bothered freight wagons trekking back to Ennis. What could be out there? Maybe a mountain lion, or sometimes black bear would wander down from the mountains. He thought about Butch Wicker being strung up, to discard the idea of a rifleman sighting in on him. Another possibility, and he grimaced worriedly at this notion, was that the owner of the Double Tree had found out about his daughter coming to see him in Ennis, and just maybe some of Tremane's cowhands were lurking along the road. He glanced at his .44-40 Winchester, which had been chambered to take revolver shells.

"Let them try something," he muttered uneasily.

While on that butte less'n a mile to the south lurked sharpshooter Adin Webb. Earlier he had viewed the passing of the freight wagons through his BOSS scope. For a moment he'd brought his Ballard & Lacy sighting in on Mickey Bellcone, with his finger tightening on the trigger before realizing his mistake. Pulling back, he'd puzzled over the absence of the man he was going to kill. Then, in the hazy distance to the west, he detected a faint spiral of smoke, laid his scope that way to determine it came from a chimney. So the man from Taney County had waited, thinking that Danny Bellcone's wagon must have broken down.

"That's Bellcone all right." Webb smiled as he sat up straighter on the English hunting seat to ease a slight cramp in his lower back. He'd left his suit coat back with the horses, had rolled up his shirt sleeves and removed his string tie. As of this moment his prey was still out of effective range. Stretching, he laid twinkling and squinting eyes up at soft billowy clouds scudding southeasterly, at ease with himself yet gripped by a killing fever.

Back on the road, the mules had settled down, though one of them kept shying into another so that all six kept veering to the north side of the hardpacked road, and with that mule's ears cocked and its head swiveling the other way as though it had sighted something. Danny Bellcone didn't want to use his whip as this would work the mules up even more.

"Something sure as heck is there."

He'd been sitting, now he stood up to study the rim of the butte, working from the west and along its ragged crestline, came about midway along the high wall, went on before his eyes suddenly froze. He'd seen something? . . . Or had it just been a heat mirage? His eyes swung back, trying to spot something his mind told him was there, that in passing before his eyes had moved on. Now he held his gaze to a certain spot high on the butte wall . . . spotted something a grayish-white color . . . and then the vague outline of a man's upper body took shape.

In one motion Danny Bellcone scooped up the Winchester and let go of the reins as he simply plunged out of the wagon and downward to hit the side of the road even as his frightened ears picked up the distant crackling of a rifle. As the mules came to an uncertain halt on the road, Danny spit road dust out of his mouth and sprang up to crouch by the wagon.

"Man's got to be loco trying to hit me from there?"

From where he crouched behind the wagon Danny knew his rig was visible to the ambusher, that from such a great distance the rifleman had to be using a scope. His first traces of fear had gone away, as had some of his worry, for he knew even for his Winchester the butte was out of rifle range. Then a slug slammed into the wagon bed to splay out wooden chips, and to have panic surge in Danny Bellcone. Glancing back over his shoulder, he saw that the first traces of tall grass were too far away, while opposite it grew tall by the road and spread carpet-like almost to the lower reaches of the butte. So without thinking too much on it he broke that way, to simply dive headfirst into the grass.

Anger made him lever a shell into the breech of his .44-40, caused him to at first crawl then come into a running crouch toward the butte. Anger and all of the pent-up bitterness he held toward Joshua Tremane kept him wanting to get within the range of his Winchester.

At first Adin Webb couldn't believe he'd missed, as his target had been less than a mile distance. One moment Danny Bellcone had been standing there, the next he'd vanished, and with the slug from Webb's gun finding only thin summery air. "Don't panic, damnit, he's ducked behind the wagon." A second firing of the Ballard and Lacy after being hastily reloaded had scoured into the wagon.

"What the hell, there's Bellcone, cutting this way through that damnable grass."

He rapped an angry knuckle against the butt of his rifle, and then calmed himself to take stock of the situation. In order to get closer to the road Adin Webb had ascended to this rocky outcropping about midway down the butte wall. To go up and come around would take too long. He could make out an ascending crevice just to his right. By taking it be could head off Bellcone, get this over with. While mulling this over he'd been reloading the rifle. This was the first time he'd actually missed, but Danny Bellcone was throwing a challenge at him the way he was coming in through the rippling prairie grass. So why not go down and pick up the gauntlet, as he figured Bellcone was toting a rifle.

Quickly the sharpshooter set the rifle down, and into his trouser pockets he shoved leaden balls, wadding patches, looped the leather strap attached to the powder horn around his neck, and picked up the ramrod and his Ballard & Lacy. The barrel alone weighed over thirty pounds, and a lot of men had a hard enough time aiming the weapon, much less packing it around. But the Missourian had little difficulty cradling the rifle in his arm as he came away from the screening rocks and picked his way downward. His unexpected appearance brought slugs from Bellcone's Winchester punching into the lower reaches of the butte and far below Adin Webb. Which caused him to hold up, to lift the rifle to his shoulder and sight in on his prey weaving through the grass.

"Bam!" The Ballard & Lacy jolted back his shoulder, and brought a curse from the man holding it. "Damned grass is fluttering too much." Then he ducked in behind a boulder and began reloading.

Out on the flats below, Danny Bellcone had felt the bullet from the Missourian's gun brush past his left arm and thud into the ground even as he realized the range was too far for his Winchester. He'd been surprised at the ambusher showing himself. And without pondering on it had levered four slugs in that direction.

"That was plumb stupid," Danny chided as he

suddenly veered to come at a different angle through the grass. "Run out of shells and you're dead."

The duel went on as Adin Webb found the base of the slope and the endless carpet of prairie grass. They exchanged shots, neither man scoring a hit, while without realizing it they'd circled away from the butte and were working their way back toward the main road. Desperately, and as the range narrowed, Danny had been firing two shots to the sharpshooter's one. He had that sixgun lodged in his holster, a useless weapon against that .50 caliber rifle. What he didn't know was of Webb's beginning to tire, to hold his rifle with arms sapped of their strength. At the moment the man from Taney County had dropped to his knees, simply let go of the Ballard & Lacy. It was an effort to wipe sweat from his brow, while his mouth gaped open as he tried to drag air into his heaving lungs, and with sweat staining his face and shirt.

"Damn it . . . can't seem to hit Bellcone . . ."

Somehow he managed to pick up his weapon and reload it. Then, in an attempt to locate his prey for a final shot, he jumped up and yelled, "Damnit, Bellcone, you're as good as dead!" Just as quickly to flop down when the other's Winchester opened up.

Danny Bellcone stared at his Winchester as if it had betrayed him when the trigger clicked on an empty chamber. Frantically he pumped the lever; again a clicking which seemed to echo the pounding of his heart and the veins at his temples. He cast frightened eyes about to get his bearings. There, the road, beyond that his wagon just drifted off it where the mules had run it against some large rocks to entangle the traces and wagon tongue, and with the mules simply standing there and with heads lowered to graze. At a crouch he ran but still grasping the Winchester, then he seemed to check himself and double up and to mutter, "Side cramped up . . . damnit . . . not now." He dropped to one knee, exhausted, and almost too spent of energy to go on or even care what happened next.

"No," Danny cried out and disregarding the pain and his tiredness of limb as he lurched upward and made for the wagon where in its bed there were more shells for his rifle. He made it there just as Adin Webb emerged from prairie grass to come in at a shambling walk.

"Been a helluva fight," chortled Webb.

Spinning to face his assailant, Danny Bellcone simply let go of his rifle to have it clatter at his feet. One of his hands grasped the wheel for support as the face of the Missourian swam before his spinning eyes stung by sweat and pure fright. "Go ahead then . . . do it . . . you damned murderer . . ."

"Easy . . . does it," gasped Adin Webb upon coming onto the road and closer to the wagon, the rifle cradled in both arms and the barrel pointing northeasterly and away from Danny.

It was then something stirred in Danny Bellcone, that what the ambusher carried was more heavy weight than weapon. That the man with the southern accent was probably more spent than he was. How much time would it take for this southerner to swing that barrel to cover him and to pull the trigger, a second, maybe two at the most. Even now Danny could feel the strength coming back into his young arms, realized at a distance of a few feet it all came down to one thing, the speed of his draw against the southerner's reaction time, and he said scornfully, "Who hired you to kill me? And I expect it wasn't Butch Wicker doing in those others either?"

"Do you really want to know, Bellcone?"

"You damned right, mister!"

"Just some rancher."

"Tremane, damn him!"

Adin Webb allowed a smile to appear, and then before his startled eyes the man he had come to kill was going for that holstered sixgun. His reaction was immediate, tired arms trying to swing the Ballard & Lacy to get this over with, but Bellcone's handgun sounding and a slug punching into his midriff, another into his chest, another—then the sharpshooter's weapon crackled. Couldn't have missed? came a puzzled thought to the Missourian. What was happening . . . the Ballard & Lacy beginning to slip out of his arms . . . why this awful weakness and the way it had gotten dark all of a sudden . . . and why couldn't he stand up. His knees jarred onto the road, and with his arms seeming to dangle helplessly at his sides. Somehow he had a smile for Danny Bellcone.

"It mus' be now de . . . de kingdom comin', . . ."

He groped to hold onto the spark of life, Webb's eyes widening in a sudden blaze of remembrance.

"An . . . an de year ob Jubilo!" A puzzled gleam came into his eyes, and then a look of utter horror twisted up his dying countenance. "No . . . you're the death angel . . . sent from . . . hell . . ."

He simply toppled forward at Danny Bellcone's feet, stirring up the dust, and only now was Danny aware of horsemen pounding in from the east. He said bitterly, "Another man dead . . . and all because of Joshua Tremane. I . . . I just can't hate like that. Man's got to let go." Retrieving his Winchester, Danny Bellcone was drinking thirstily from his canteen when the lawmen found him.

Chapter Nineteen

For a long time everyone held a grudge against the Double Tree and Melissa Tremane. It got so that she rarely ventured into town, and then two years after Joshua Tremane had been gunned down by Sheriff Ben Taylor, Melissa simply turned the running of the ranch over to Sid Mason and left for an unknown eastern city. She saw Danny Bellcone only one time after he had killed the man from Taney County, a brief interlude in Ennis. At the time he hadn't known her father had hired Adin Webb. But at the time it wouldn't have made any difference as Danny Bellcone sold out his interest in the freight wagons and caught the morning stage without looking her up to say goodbye.

Danny and his brother, Mickey, took that long promised trip to Butte. For Danny it was to buy a half-interest in a hardware store, while Mickey Bellcone couldn't stand working in the mines and quit to head into Idaho. Six months later Danny sold out, but instead of looking up his brother in Idaho he found that much to his surprise he was aboard an eastbound train.

Detraining at Bozeman, he shed the clothing of a businessman for that worn by a working cowhand and a horse and saddle and pointed the bronc in a southerly direction. He avoided the stagecoach relay stations on the Bozeman to Madison Valley run by camping out along creeks or in deserted cabins. At last, when the valley opened up before him, Danny took boldly to the stagecoach road. Now it became more clear to him why he'd come back not only to pay his respects at the graves of his parents but to see again a place holding so many bittersweet memories. Maybe he'd run into Link Cavanaugh or Olsen or Art Dickey, others he'd freighted with. While the last person he expected to see was Melissa Tremane. Or it could be she was part of the reason he was here, getting a glimpse of Ennis now, and striking toward the cowtown looking just as it always had.

Three years could change a man, as Danny Bellcone had filled out more, had taken to wearing a mustache. A few names, he noticed, had changed up front of some business places, and the streets weren't as packed as before, and there were few faces he could put a name to. Yet there ahead on his right was the Moonlight Tavern, and he veered the bronc toward it as of a man sighting a waterhole out in the Mojave. Coming up to one of the hitching rails, he was swinging down when several horsemen and a carriage swept out of a side street.

His eyes taking in the brands on the horses,

Danny said bitterly, "That Double Tree bunch." He thought about Joshua Tremane passing away just before he'd left, felt no traces of remorse. He tied up and turned his back on the riders as a boot found the boardwalk, only to have someone call out to him. Swiveling a glance back, Danny saw that it was Sid Mason reining his carriage to this side of the street. And Danny turned and held there when Mason drove up and got out of the carriage.

"Well, Mr. Mason, it's been a long time," he said matter-of-factly.

"It has, Danny."

"If you'll excuse me . . ."

"Danny, we've got to talk."

"As I recall before," he shot back, "any talking done by the Double Tree was with a fist."

"That kind of thing is dead and buried now, Danny. You weren't the only one Tremane wanted done in. My name was on that list too."

"You—why'd he want to kill you?"

"It'll be more private in the Moonlight."

"An' what list are you talking about?" Somewhat reluctantly he followed Sid Mason into the saloon, where they commandeered a bottle of whiskey and a back table.

At sixty-two Sid Mason was showing his years. He had on a woolen cattleman's coat and his hat pushed back to unshade his washed-out blue eyes. About him was the easy look of a man contented with what life had done to him. He filled their shot glasses and said, "In this town the name Bellcone means a lot."

Startled by what Mason had just said, Danny gazed into the man's steady eyes, suddenly realized Sid Mason wasn't just tossing around some patronizing words. "It wasn't always that way."

"I expect if you hadn't killed that sharpshooter, Mr. Bellcone, I just might not be here talking to you today. Still get chills thinking on it. Not so much him gunning me down, but of Joshua Tremane's part in this."

"You worked for Tremane . . . ever . . . ever since I was born, it seems."

"It wasn't Joshua so much as this disease that was killing him. Wasn't in his right mind the last few years. So as to why I'm here talking to you, Danny. Meaning there's still Melissa."

"How . . . is she?"

"Coming home, Danny. Still not married—and still mooning over a certain young man." Around sipping at the whiskey and low words he spoke to Danny Bellcone, there came from cattleman Sid Mason the story of why Melissa's father wanted these men killed. "So you see, Danny, Melissa has a cross to bear too. Reason I'm out there running the ranch for her. And reason she's coming home is she's tired of running . . . away from herself and the past."

"Guess then, Mr. Mason, she'll marry this young man. Wish her well."

"Stage is due most anytime, Danny. Why don't we mosey out and watch it roll in."

"Nope, I'd just be in the way," he said wistfully.

"Obliged for all you told me, Sid, and the drinks."

"Son, it's you I'm talking about."

"I don't follow you?"

Once again Danny Bellcone found himself accompanying Sid Mason through a doorway, but outside this time and upstreet to where others were gathered near the stagecoach office. Her letters, explained Mason as they stepped along, always spoke of Danny Bellcone, of where her heart would always be.

When the stagecoach suddenly came rolling in from the north, the six horses coming on at a canter, Danny had this sudden urge to bolt out of here and strike for his bronc. He was conscious of other Double Tree hands mingled in the crowd, but when the stage got closer, all he could do was stand there rooted to the ground alongside Sid Mason. This was all a dream, came a whispery voice in his mind. He half-expected to see Old Anse Pickard up there with the driver just reining up his horses, then an older couple dismounted first, followed by a suave-looking gent in a vested suit, who immediately swung back to extend a helping hand to another passenger.

"My pleasure, Miss Tremane."

"As it is mine," laughed Melissa Tremane. Stepping down from the high step, she removed her bonnet and fluttered out her hair as Sid Mason came up to embrace her. "Oh, Sid, how good it is to be home."

"That's double for me and the rest of us. Remember telling me what your heart's desire would be?"

"Just being home is enough, Sid."

Gently he put a hand on her arm to bring Melissa's eyes sweeping along the fringes of those crowding the boardwalk. She came to Danny Bellcone, and simply froze, her eyes riveted to his face. But from where he stood Danny Bellcone could see the disbelieving glaze break away to have shimmer in her eyes the inner thoughts of Melissa Tremane.

Unmindful of where he was and of those watching, he lifted away his hat and stepped toward the woman he loved. "I . . . I heard you were coming home." He brushed a tear away from her uplifted face. "Been some time since I've seen anyone as lovely." To his surprise she brought her arms up to encircle his neck, and to have him brush more tears away.

"Danny, you're here."

"Reckon I am at that."

"Will you be staying long?"

"As long as you want—and maybe longer."